ANN RINALDI

My Vicksburg

Harcourt
Houghton Mifflin Harcourt
BOSTON   NEW YORK
2009

Requests for permission to make copies of any part of the work should be
submitted online at www.harcourt.com/contact or mailed to the following address:
Permissions Department, Houghton Mifflin Harcourt Publishing Company, Inc.,
6277 Sea Harbor Drive, Orlando, Florida 32887-6777.

Harcourt is an imprint of Houghton Mifflin Harcourt Publishing Company.
www.hmhbooks.com

Library of Congress Cataloging-in-Publication Data
Rinaldi, Ann.
My Vicksburg / Ann Rinaldi. — 1st ed.
p. cm.
Summary: During the siege of Vicksburg, thirteen-year-old Claire Louise struggles with
difficult choices when family and friends join opposing sides of the war.
ISBN 978-0-15-206624-6 (hardcover)
1. Vicksburg (Miss.)–History–Siege, 1863–Juvenile fiction. [1. Vicksburg (Miss.)–History–
Siege, 1863–Fiction. 2. United States–History–Civil War, 1861-1865–Fiction. 3. Brothers
and sisters–Fiction. 4. Family life–Mississippi–Fiction. 5. Friendship–Fiction.] I. Title.
PZ7.R459Myv 2009
[Fic]–dc22   2008020852

Text set in Adobe Garamond

Printed in the United States of America

QUM 10 9 8 7 6 5 4 3 2 1

To Cindy, a tried and true friend

CHAPTER ONE

May 1863
Vicksburg, Mississippi

THE ONLY reason we came back to town, and stayed during that terrible nightmare of a time, those forty-seven days of confusion and heartbreak that made up the siege of Vicksburg, was because of Sammy the cat.

Oh, other people stayed, for other reasons, mostly because they couldn't believe it was all happening. "It will go away," they told themselves. "The Yankees will soon understand that they made a mistake coming here. What's here for them, anyway?

"And until that realization comes to those Blue Coats, we'll just build ourselves some caves to live in, to protect ourselves from the cannon fire, the rifled artillery, the exploding missiles, and the general pandemonium all around us.

"And we'll eat beans and rice and bacon and corn-meal. And maybe, when all that runs out, maybe rats and mule meat." That's what the people said.

When we heard the first firing, on Sunday, May 17, we were just outside a small town called Bolton's Depot, at Fruitvale, Pa's parents' plantation. We'd been there for a little over two weeks, ever since General Grant and his army crossed the Mississippi and landed at a Confederate stronghold below the mouth of the Big Black River.

Here at Fruitvale we had commodious rooms, the best horses to ride, servants galore. And Mama had brought along all Pa's medical books and her home remedy books, for her home remedies worked side by side with Pa's modern doctor ways. She also brought her good dresses and jewelry, and mine and James's going-to-church clothes.

My little brother, James, who was only five, said he could hear the artillery shells from way down at Big Black River where the Yankees were fighting and getting closer to Vicksburg.

James was afraid for Sammy, who was back home in Vicksburg.

"What you're hearing is the mortar bombs from Porter's fleet on the river below the bluffs," Pa explained to him. "We're safe here."

"But Sammy isn't. He's home alone in our house."

"Clothilda and Andy are with him."

"That's worse," James said. "They won't let him cuddle next to them at night and he needs somebody." He was trying not to cry. At five it isn't easy.

I know. I'm thirteen and it isn't easy.

"He'll be all right," Mama soothed James. He was her "little man." She called him that, and for the most part he lived up to it. But I envied him for still being able to break into tears when the occasion warranted it. I, myself, was too old. Anyway, Pa would be put out with me if I cried. And the last thing in the world I wanted was for Pa to be put out with me.

He expected me to be a young lady, a comfort to Mama and him, what with my older brother Landon off to war for six months now, home only once, in April.

It would be all nice and fit and proper and we would be the typical Southern family and I would be knitting socks and sending them to Landon, except for one thing.

Landon had gone and joined up with the wrong side.

Landon was with the Yankees, with Grant. Oh, he wasn't out there this minute fighting his way to destroy our town. He was with Grant, all right. But, like Pa, Landon was a doctor. His was the first class to study under the president of Harvard, Charles Eliot. He had completed written exams, clinical sciences, and a three-year degree program.

"Should have never sent you there," Pa had scolded him when he came home in his blue Yankee uniform with the double row of buttons down the front. "You learned more than medicine. You learned their sentiments, their ideals, their beliefs. Did you get extra credit for all that?"

Pa was as mad as a wet porcupine. I think I even saw tears crowding his eyes when he looked across the supper table at his pride and joy in that blue uniform. He'd been so proud of Landon up until now. He'd had plans for after the war, of Landon working with him in his surgery.

"I'm not going to be shooting Confederates, Pa," Landon said. "I will likely be treating them if they come my way. You know how I feel about killing. The same as you."

Pa had had nothing to say about that. He knew Landon spoke the truth.

"If I embarrass you in this uniform, sir," Landon said quietly, "well, I won't come home anymore. I don't want to hurt your standing in this town."

"Yes, and that kind of talk is what will get you run out of the house, as far as your mother and I are concerned," Pa said. "You're a doctor. You do us proud. You just haven't got the brains to know which side to serve. Now the conversation is over."

Pa worried about him. I know he did. Sometimes I caught him sitting there staring into the middle distance, a book in his hands, and I knew he was thinking of Landon, though he never spoke of him.

Mama did. She called him "my boy." She kept his boyhood room as he'd left it. She waited for his letters and read them to us at the supper table. Pa said nothing when she read them.

Now in the parlor at Fruitvale, James ran to Pa and hugged his leg. "I want to go *hoooo*me."

Mama's eyes were tearing up now, too. "Please, can we, Hugh? I miss home. I miss my things."

"You've brought many of them with you," he reminded her.

In the last two weeks we'd heard the news from neighbors who'd left town and passed Fruitvale. Forts were springing up on the bluffs of Vicksburg, above the Mississippi. An 18-pound cannon the army had set up on the bluff was named "Whistling Dick."

And finally the words we never thought we'd hear: "The Yankees are coming!"

"CLAIRE LOUISE, take your brother into the kitchen and give him some cookies and milk," Pa directed me.

I did so. There was nothing like cookies and milk to dry James's tears. And I promised to play chess with him, though I found myself missing home, too. Our house was on Cherry Street, a pleasant street of cobblestones lined with trees. It is more pleasant than imposing, made of white clapboard, welcoming and commodious. The river is to the west of us.

From the front parlor now I could hear my parents' voices rising and falling in a lively discussion. But I could not hear the words.

"Do you think Mama will tell Pa to take us back?" James asked.

"She doesn't *tell* him what to do," I corrected him. "They talk things over first. And that's what they're doing now. Don't forget, Pa's going away. He won't be here to protect us. And he wants to make sure we're all right before he goes. He wants to do right by us, James."

He nodded, wordlessly.

It occurred to me that the chess set was in the front

parlor, where my parents were. I told James I had to fetch it and went out into the wide hall, wide enough to house a whole regiment. I stood, for a moment, outside the door of the front parlor and heard them negotiating.

"That's it," Pa was saying. "You promise to live in the cave I've prepared for you and the children and we'll go back. There's no other way I'll allow it, Louisa." I recognized the voice he used. Steady and firm, like he often used on me.

"With my home standing within plain sight? You want me to live in a *cave?*" Mama asked.

There was a moment's silence. Which could mean he was holding her and kissing her. My pa was usually a private man when it came to displaying affection to Mama. I'd never, except for a kiss on her forehead, seen him exhibit tenderness. I'd always supposed they did that sort of thing in private.

"I'm sorry, Louisa. But the house is a target. At least, underground, you all have a chance." His voice was muffled. He was kissing her now, I imagined.

My pa is a good-looking man. His full head of hair is streaked with iron gray, his shoulders broad, his waist still lean. His jaw is firm, too firm sometimes. His nose is straight and strong, his eyebrows heavy and his mouth too often unyielding. When he looks at you, you pay mind. And there are times you wish he didn't look at you. Usually, though, a look is enough to put you on notice.

Mama adores him. I know he is a man of good parts.

And I also know that, even being a man of good parts, he does not approve of me. I do not know the reason why. He never says the reason why. I wish he would. Even though, at the same time, I understand that he leaves it to me to figure out. Because he knows that only when I comprehend why he does not approve of me will I be able to mend my ways and gain his approval.

I lay awake sometimes studying on it. Sometimes I cry. He dotes on James. His hopes are all tied up in Landon even though he went and joined up with the Yankees. Me? I am the wrong one. The outsider. *I do not belong.* He is ever kindly to me, but it is tinged with sternness.

"And? If Landon comes home?" I heard Mama saying behind closed doors. "Am I permitted to invite him into this cave?" Oh, Mama knew how to play her cards, all right.

"If Landon comes home, have him check on the gash I stitched up on the head of little Jimmy Otis. And tell him that Mrs. Otis is with child again and has to take her special medicine."

"So you're going to work in concert with him anyway? Your Yankee son."

"He's a darned good doctor. Came in top of his class at Harvard."

"You've forgiven him then?"

"Can't let him know it. Not yet. Not right." More silence.

I heard Mama sigh. "Oh, Hugh, I don't want you to go. I want things back the way they were."

"We never get that in life, Louisa. The now is all we get. So you promise to live in the cave with the children then?"

"Yes." Her voice was tearful. "And Sammy the cat, too?"

"Yes," he said wearily, "and Sammy the cat."

We left that very afternoon in the dray with Chip, Pa's "man," driving the wagon and Easter, whom we'd brought from home, driving the surrey. On the road we met all kinds of people fleeing the town. Only we, the Corbets of Cherry Street, were going back to the town.

And all because of Sammy the cat.

CHAPTER TWO

IF JAMES had his cat to worry about, I had my friend, Amy.

After all, she was my best friend, and I'd promised to stay with her through it all. Then what had I done?

Fickle-boots me, I'd run away. I'd left town, that's what I'd done. Just when Amy needed me the most.

Oh, before we'd left to go to Grandma's, I'd asked Pa if I could stay with the Clarkes. I'd be safe with them, I told him. But he'd said no. You didn't say anything back when Pa said no like that. Not that he'd shouted it or anything. Pa did not have to shout. At his age, which was forty-six, I calculate, he'd done all the shouting a man had to do to have the world know he was someone to be reckoned with.

As a doctor with a going practice in town, people knew him as soft-spoken and sure of himself. They trusted him and he returned that trust in full.

As for we, his children, Pa was more available for his patients than he was for us. Oh, he did right by us. However, there were times when we thought he didn't know we were alive. But just do something we weren't supposed to do, and we found out he was very much aware that we were alive.

Just be bad enough in school so it warranted a note home (me).

Just throw something of Mama's across the room (James).

Just go and join the *other* army (Landon).

And, of a sudden, Pa was out of his surgery, which was attached to the white, rambling house with the porch in front, and he was in the parlor, calling you before him. And still, though he didn't raise his voice one octave, you were asked something like: "Did I have to leave Jimmy Otis with a three-inch cut in his head for *this?*"

And of course you said nosir. You answered properlike. Even though James would cry and reach out his arms to be comforted. It must have torn Pa to pieces not to be able to soothe the little fellow until he was finished scolding.

I *wanted* to cry, but dared not. I usually hiccuped instead. He'd order me to stop hiccuping, even though he knew I couldn't. So, disgusted with me, he'd send me to the cellar for the rest of the afternoon. The *cellar*, where all my demons came to join me. I was terrified of the cellar and Pa knew it. If Landon was home, he'd come and join me.

Landon, now, he'd take his just deserts, yessir and nosir Pa to death, and go sullenly into a cellar of his own making, chastising himself more than Pa ever could.

The point is we all adored Pa. He knew it. And he very much knew we were alive and thinking and plotting and doing all sorts of things that young people do when they are struggling to figure out their place in the world. Or at least in Vicksburg.

Now, he was leaving us.

He and I had a serious talk at my grandparents' plantation just before we left. Pa had already put on the uniform of a Confederate major and, oh, it made it difficult for me to look up at him, what with the mustard-colored sash and the sword and the high boots and the epaulets on his shoulders.

If I was sometimes put off by my father, I was outright afraid of him in this uniform. He was now with the 2nd Mississippi Regiment going to join up with Lee on his move north, headed to Pennsylvania. No more would he stitch up a three-inch cut on a little boy's head. Now he would have to cut off a leg or an arm on a grown man.

"I have no doubt you'd have been safe with the Clarkes," he told me. "They're good people. It isn't that. It's that we have to stay together as a family. I'm looking to you to help keep the family together, Claire Louise. Landon has gone off to join forces with the devil, and I'm leaving tomorrow. I expect you to be a comfort to your mother and to look after your little brother. The Clarkes are sticking together, aren't they?"

I can lie as good as the next one when the occasion warrants it. "Yessir," I said.

"Be careful of the older girl. Sarah. There's something going on with her," he said. "And I think it's more than just romancing Landon."

I looked at him quickly. "What?"

"I'm not talking out of school if I tell you that she came to my surgery to have a mole removed from her face. Said she didn't want to be recognized by it. I laughingly asked her if she was going to be a spy for the Confederacy, and she didn't answer. Just be careful and don't be influenced by anything she says. All right?"

"Yessir," I said again.

And there it was in a nutshell, why Amy needed me. Her older sister, Sarah, who was seventeen, was going to give her family trouble.

Sarah was joining the Southern army. As a man. She was going for a soldier. And only Amy and I knew it. Landon didn't know it before he left. Oh no, Landon could not be told, or he'd never have gone. Sarah had decided that.

Riding in the surrey with Mama and James on the way back to Vicksburg, with Pa alongside us on his black stallion, Mercer, I worried. Had Sarah Clarke left yet as a soldier? If so, what did she tell her family? Did they know? Or did only Amy know? Oh, I must be allowed to be excused as soon as we got home to go next door and see her.

I was still thinking of home as it was when we left it, with its pristine houses and church spires and view of the river in the distance. When we got close to the Joe Davis plantation (he is the brother of President Jefferson Davis), we first heard the firing of the cannon, which we soon learned was the battle of Champion Hill.

Cannon fire soon filled the air, and James began to

cry. Pa reached over from Mercer's back and took James onto the saddle with him. Pa had a special place in his heart for James.

My one wish in life was to find my special place in Pa's heart. Times I saw him eyeing me with a fondness when he didn't think I saw. But then Pa would say something jagged, covered by humor, that cut like a scalpel.

Mama said he did not know how to act with me at my sensitive age. "When was the last time he took you on his lap?" she asked.

Tears came to my eyes. I could not remember.

"He doesn't want you to grow up," she told me. "He doesn't know what to do with you now that you are growing up. So he teases you."

"He's always telling me to grow up."

"He means behave. He is more comfortable," she said, "with his sons. So he gets brusque and stern. He dies a little inside, thinking of the boys he someday may have to share you with."

"Mama, I'm only thirteen. Why punish me for it now?"

"He knows what's coming."

It sounded right, but it was not right. Not by my calculations. Pa was a doctor. He should know, more than anybody, what a girl went through when she was growing up, and what love she needed from her own father. And he was not giving it. And now he was leaving.

As we got closer to Vicksburg, the road before us

became crowded with soldiers—Confederate soldiers, ragged and some barefoot, with dirty faces and hollow eyes and shamefaced looks. They stopped and saluted when they saw Pa.

"We been beat, sir. The enemy is pursuing us from Big Black and Bridgeport Ferry."

"Never mind that," Pa said. "I understand there are Louisiana and Tennessee troops commanding the riverfront. So we're still strong. Vicksburg won't fall. Now, is anybody here hurt?

One man had a slash on his head and Pa stopped, took his doctor's bag right out of the surrey, and fixed the head right there. Then we went on.

It was night by the time we got to Vicksburg. Fierce shelling was going on from Porter's ironclad boats on the river. It was like fireworks on the Fourth of July. We didn't go home. Home was across town, Pa said, and he wouldn't let us go there. We went, instead, inside a church. The street outside was crowded with wagons, caissons, artillery, surreys, and waiting horses. I think it was the Catholic Church, St. Paul's, on the corner of Crawford and Walnut streets. We weren't Catholic, but Pa knew we would be welcome. He took us to the basement, where it was lighted with tall candles and people were sleeping in pews and on the floor.

Soldiers and families. Up front was a grotto with the Virgin Mary in it. It was deep and looked like it was made with real rocks and it scared me. But I have friends in school who are Catholic and they tell me that if you are of that religion you are supposed to be scared, about everything.

That goes against the grain of my family, who teach us not to be frightened of anything, that if we are right and good, nothing bad can happen to us.

There were soldiers sleeping all over on the floor of the grotto. It seemed as if the Virgin Mary was watching them . . .

Pa went and spoke with the priest. He came back and found us a place in a corner and we settled on a rug near the confessional. He covered us with blankets Mama had brought from our grandparents. James was sleeping already.

"I'm told there's a woman having a baby upstairs," he said to Mama. "I've got to see to her."

Then, without caring who was looking, he took Mama in his arms and kissed her like they'd just been married. And held her close. And whispered something so low even I couldn't hear.

Mama nodded and he held her that way for a long moment.

He released her and looked down at me, quizzically. "You get the urge, confess your sins," he said solemnly. "The priest is right over there."

There was the humor again. Covering what? What did he want to say? "I've got no sins," I said.

He looked down at me for a long minute, taking my

measure until I became uncomfortable. What was coming next? "Only God knows different," he said. "And me."

I said nothing. What did he know? What had I done?

"Get up when I'm speaking to you," he said.

Oh Lord, not here, not now. What *had* I done?

I stood before him.

"Don't you know you're supposed to stand in the presence of your commanding officer?" he asked.

"Yessir," I said.

He took off my bonnet and dropped it on the floor. He kissed me on the forehead. He looked into my face as if searching a map to find his way somewhere. Then he tenderly brushed some hair away from my face and tucked it behind my ear.

"Kiss your pa," he ordered.

I stood on tiptoe and kissed the side of his face. He hugged me, picking me up off my feet to do so. It was a hug that needed no words. A hug that said everything. I didn't think he'd ever let me go.

Then he set me down on my feet, and, without looking at me, told me roughly that I had best behave while he was gone, and take care of Mama, and if he heard anything to the contrary I would not sit down for a week.

He'd never spanked me. He was making up for his display of affection. I said, "Yessir."

In the next minute he was gone. And if I had sins, I knew they were forgiven.

CHAPTER THREE

THE NEXT morning the good sisters of the church gave us coffee and bread and butter, and it never tasted so wonderful to me in my life.

Pa was gone. He'd left at first light, Mama said, and I felt his loss like a hole inside me. I felt his unseen presence worse. Who would direct us, scold us, tell us to mind? Mama had all she could do to manage herself and the servants.

Easter helped her gather up the blankets, and we took our leave of the church. The nuns had said there were times when we could go outside without chance of being killed.

Life had come down to that, it seemed. Those times were an hour at eight in the morning, an hour at noon, and an hour at eight at night, when the Union artillerymen ate their meals.

We waited until noon and then drove across town to our house, which hadn't been destroyed yet. Mama couldn't control James, who leaped from the surrey and ran up the front steps of the house, and nearly into

Clothilda's arms. She and her husband, Andy, had been keeping the place while we were gone.

"Where is he? Where's Sammy?" James demanded.

"Good Lord, chile, he's out back, takin' in God's good sunlight," Clothilda said.

James bounded through the center hall and out the back door. "Sammy, Sammy, I'm home. I'm here. You don't have to be frightened anymore."

Mama shook her head in despair. "Tell me how that boy is going to live in a cave." Then to Clothilda, "We have to go to the cave my husband prepared for us."

"I know, ma'am," Clothilda agreed. "He wuz here early this mornin' and gave us instructions. We all ready."

"God bless that man," Mama said fervently. "Now we have less than an hour before the artillery begins again. Quickly, let's get some things together."

"Most of it be together already." Clothilda pointed to the stack of parcels across the hall in the front parlor— blankets and pillows, sheets and towels, boxes filled with kitchen supplies. "There be food in barrels out on the back porch," Clothilda told Mama. "Andy be gettin' the sides o' ham."

I saw tears in Mama's eyes. "I must assemble my remedies in a box," she said.

The windows of the house were open and I heard voices from next door. Amy and her sister.

The last I'd spoken with her, Amy had told me her father had hinted that they might go to Jackson if the Yankees came. They had people in Jackson.

"Claire Louise, put the blankets and sheets into the wagon," Mama ordered.

I did so and now I had some extra time. But I also had a dilemma.

Should I go to the barn and say hello to my horse, Jewel? And tell her how sorry I was that I hadn't taken her to Grandmother's? I'd wanted to take her, but Pa said no. Grandmother had enough horses, and Andy would care for her.

Or should I slip through the hedges that separated our property and go to the Clarkes'? I more or less owed that to Landon. He'd asked me to keep him apprised of Sarah Clarke's welfare.

To put it in a delicate way, Landon was daft over Sarah. I knew they'd had some sort of falling out before he'd left, but I didn't know why.

"Mama, can I go next door and visit Amy?"

"No. I need you."

I DIDN'T bother knocking on the front door. Amy and I were that close. Her mother, Virginia, passed me in the hall. "Back, are you? How is your mother faring? Did your papa leave yet? Where did you all sleep last night? Do you all have a cave assigned to you?"

She did go on, that woman. And she never waited for an answer. Never expected one. Just kept on with what she was about. I know she drove Landon to distraction sometimes. But he'd resigned himself to just yes-ma'aming and no-ma'aming her to death.

I went on upstairs where I found Amy and Sarah. They were bundling some clothes into a pillowcase for Sarah.

"Claire Louise, you're back!" Amy near screamed it.

She and I hugged, and she inquired where we were going to stay. "Neither of our houses has been hit yet," she said. "But Pa says we are going to Jackson anyway. Oh, Claire Louise, I don't want to go! I don't want to be parted from you!"

She was crying, and now I started in, too.

Sarah just stood by. I noticed her hair was cut short. It should have detracted from her looks, but it didn't. It made her prettier, if you ask me, more elfin looking. And she had beautiful large blue eyes. I think, I told myself, that she must have broken my brother's heart by now.

I noticed she had on boots and a man's trousers and shirt. And there was no mole on her face.

"Where are you going in those clothes?" I pretended ignorance.

"To Washington," she said. "To be a nurse. Clara Barton needs nurses."

Even if I hadn't already known the truth I'd have seen that for a lie. I ought to recognize one—I tell enough of them. Out of the corner of my eye I saw Amy roll her eyes and shake her head, no.

"Why don't you tell the truth, Sarah?" she asked her sister. "You're running off to join the Confederate army like a man!"

Sarah flushed. "I suppose you went and told everyone!"

"Only Claire Louise. And only because I thought she might be able to talk you out of it."

Sarah tossed her head like any seventeen-year-old would. Like I wished I could. "If she had such special power, why didn't she talk her brother out of joining the Yankee army, I ask you?"

I felt my face go red. "Is that why you two argued before he left?"

"Yes. Part of it. I'm not going to wed a turncoat. And be known all over town as the wife of that Landon Corbet. The one who turned his back on his people. And anyway, I don't want to wait until the war is over to wed. I want to do it now."

Amy and I looked at each other and burst out in laughter. "You just contradicted yourself," Amy told her. "You won't marry a turncoat, but you wanted to marry him before he left."

Sarah burst out in tears and flung herself into Amy's arms. Her sister held her and then I joined them, wrapping my arms around them.

Sarah drew away and wiped her eyes with the sleeve of her shirt. "Oh, I hate that brother of yours, Claire Louise. And at the same time I love him so much I could die. Do you know what a dream he is?"

I shook my head, no. "He's just my brother," I told her.

"You write to him, don't you?"

I said I did.

"Then you can do me a favor. Tell him I ran away and joined the *Confederate* army. I want to punish him for thinking he can have everything his way."

Amy was horrified. "Is *that* why you're going to fight like a man?"

"Yes," Sarah snapped. "I'm joining Lee in the Cumberland Valley."

"You have to go all the way out there?" Amy scolded. "Why not right here where we're fighting for our town?"

"I'd be recognized," Sarah returned.

In the stunned silence that followed we heard my mother calling up the stairs.

"Claire Louise? Are you up there?"

"Yes, Mama."

"When I said you couldn't come here? You wait until I tell your father about this. He'll give you what for. Now you come down this minute, young lady. We're leaving for the cave. The shelling is about to start. Claire Louise, if you don't come this instant I'll have to come up there and get you. And then you'll be sorry."

Mama's threats were empty. She never knew what to do to make me sorry.

Amy kissed me. "Go," she said.

The enormity of the situation hung over us like a sword.

We both knew we might never see each other again.

Both of us loved and wept over English novels. Especially Jane Austen. But this, now, was worse than anything she could dream up. Or write. And we knew it.

We just looked at each other. "Be careful," I told her.

The words were so empty, and I knew it.

She nodded her promise. We hugged. I went downstairs to my waiting mama.

As IT turned out, Mama knew exactly where our cave was, and so did Chip, Pa's personal man. Chip wasn't his usual happy self. He had wanted, he told Mama, to go with Pa, to "tend to him whilst he was doin' his business of doctorin'" but Pa had said no, he'd rather have Chip home with his family. To take care of them.

Chip and Easter were to live in the cave with us. Clothilda and Andy were staying in our house, to guard it. And if it got hit, why they'd take refuge with other servants, wherever that might be, but still keep an eye on the house so it wouldn't be ransacked.

"You can't buy servants like this," Mama whispered to me, forgetting that Pa had, indeed, bought them. Likely down in New Orleans. He never spoke about things like that.

Our cave, the one Pa had had built for us, was located on a very high hill in the northeastern part of the town. You went in and there were arched hallways leading to rooms. And you could stand up in both the hallways and the rooms. Most people, I later came to understand, couldn't even stand up in their caves.

Chip brought in the bedding and the other necessities

for living. Pa had had planks laid on the floor so we wouldn't be walking on dirt.

"Can I bring Sammy in?" James asked.

"Yes," Mama said. "And keep him in. Or someone might steal him."

She did not say for what. Neither did I. But we'd heard, already, that there would be a shortage of food soon. And that people should not let their dogs and cats wander loose. Hungry soldiers would eat anything.

CHAPTER FOUR

O UR CAVE was about half a mile from town, and not too far from the Yankees. I heard firing all the way down from where the graveyard was. From Yankee entrenchments. Shells and balls fell all around us even as we were getting into the cave.

On top of the floors, especially in the bedrooms and parlor, were Persian carpets. Pa had ordered all this, and Andy and Clothilda carried out his wishes.

It was the nearest to home as they could make it. And Mama cried when she saw it and realized what he had done for us.

Easter had set up a cooking area just outside the cave, because there was no ventilation inside. There were no windows. She made a pot of coffee that evening for us, during the break at eight o'clock, and we were able to go outside and see our own soldiers marching by because we were not far from the main road. They looked good, hearty and not downcast, and I could have watched them all evening, except that soon the shelling started again and

Mama called me and James inside to help her make cartridges on the kitchen table.

"It's the least we can do. A captain from the 26th Louisiana Infantry will be by to pick them up in the morning. He's the one who left the black powder and all the fixings."

We worked until about eleven that night and made a whole pile of musket cartridges. Then we had a visitor.

Andy, from home. He stood there in the entrance hall. "Ma'am."

"Yes, Andy. Would you like some coffee? How did you get here with all the shelling?"

He gave a slow smile. I noticed for the first time that his hair was graying on top. He'd been with us as long as I could remember. Chip came in then and stood just behind him. Deferring always to Andy, even though Chip was Pa's personal man. "They's firing Parrott guns now from the peninsula across the way," Andy told us, "but I got enough 'sperience so's I know how to dodge 'em. Ma'am, I come to ask your opinion and tell you something not so good."

"Yes, Andy." Mama stood up. She was ready for anything.

There was a pause. Andy twisted his hat in his hands. "Well, you know our army gots about seven hundred mules. An' we gots no food for 'em. So we're givin' 'em over to the Yankees, 'cause they can feed 'em. I tell you this 'cause you all are gonna be seein' 'em driven right by on this highway on the way to the Yankees' camp tomorrow."

"You mean we're giving *all* our mules to the Yankees?" Mama asked.

"Just about," Andy said. "But that's not the bad part. Some horses, too. No corn is to be issued for the horses. Except for those in the field."

Silence. I held my breath because I knew what was coming. So did Mama.

"There be no officers here for Diamond and Jewel. So we get no corn. And our supply is taken by the army. We can't buy any or steal it. So I wanted to ask what you want me to do with 'em, ma'am. The horses, that is. And that means the carriage horses, too."

"We can take them to Grandma's, Mama," I intervened. "I can ride Jewel there, and Andy can take Diamond. We can lead the carriage horses."

"Quiet, Claire Louise." I'm sure Mama did not mean to be so sharp. "I need to think," she said. And in a moment she had thought it out.

"What word did my husband leave with you about the horses?" Mama asked Andy.

He looked at the floor. "That no matter what, no harm was to come to them. And not to let them starve. Shoot them first, he said. Or give them away."

"Nooo!" I wailed.

"Claire Louise!" Now she did mean to be sharp.

"Yes, ma'am," I said.

"So you know what you must do then, Andy. Take Chip with you when you bring them to the Yankees tomorrow. Wait, I'll write a note for you to give to an officer. Claire Louise, get me paper and pen."

It took me some time, but I found the required paper and pen and ink. And in a few moments Mama had penned the note that would ensure that the four horses would go to good officers and be treated well. From a respected officer and doctor in the Confederate army. And that, if alive after the war, she told where they should be returned.

She gave the note to Andy.

"I believe I'll go there tomorrow at eight when the shelling stops. I know the back paths, out of the way of the Yankees, ma'am," he said. "We'll get 'em there safe. And we'll be back soon's we're finished."

I begged to be allowed to go. Mama said no. I begged to be allowed to at least say good-bye to Jewel. Mama said no to that, too. I was sent to bed with warm milk, and Mama put something in it to make me sleep. I dreamed it was Sunday morning and Pa and I were riding out early down to the river and the sun was shining and the sky was blue and he was telling me about how it was when he was in Harvard.

CHAPTER FIVE

IT WAS Sammy the cat who woke me the next morning before the dark had even lifted. He climbed on my bed and rubbed his face against mine and purred. Which meant he wanted to go out.

"Out" from the cave meant he had to be accompanied. I blinked my eyes and sat up to light the candle beside my bed. The cave was filled with the sound of breathing, mixed with the sound I'd heard in my sleep all night, the sound of musket and cannon fire, which I'd become used to by now as one becomes accustomed to the chiming of a grandfather clock in one's own house.

The shelling is always the most fierce at dawn, Andy had told us. One battery after another opens up. I patted Sammy's black, glossy fur. He was kneading my blanket with his white paws now. Sometimes I thought Sammy was just too smart for his own good. It seemed he had a vocabulary.

"All right, all right," I told him. "Let me get dressed."

Quickly I put on my clothes. I'd wear the same dress as yesterday. Amy's mother had told mine that prices were already outlandish, that a simple calico dress was forty dollars. Mama said we had to ration everything.

As I laced up my boots I tried to figure out why I had such a thread of deep sadness running through me. What had happened yesterday to make me mourn so? And then, in a flash, it came back.

Jewel. Gone. The full thrust of it washed over me. Where was she now? Being given breakfast by some Yankee officer? I hoped he would pat her nose and find out how she loved carrots. Oh, I mustn't think of her now. Where would I go this morning with Sammy? And how would I get there? Yes, I'd think of that.

It came to me then. Thinking of Jewel made me remember it.

We'd go down to the stream where I used to ride with Pa of a Sunday morning. Why, the blackberries would be out in great plenty by now. I'd pick some. We needed a treat. I know we had enough flour for Mama to make some biscuits. Then, just as I was plotting what I was going to do, a strange thing happened.

The shelling stopped.

An eerie silence set in. And then I remembered. Yesterday our General Pemberton had sent out a flag of truce so the Yankees would have a chance to bury their dead soldiers. This must be the agreed-upon time to do the sad task. Good. Sammy and I wouldn't have to worry about the shells for at least three or four hours.

I told Sammy to come along, and we crept out the

main hall and into the kitchen, where I took up a two-quart pail and then went to the main entrance as quietly as I could, only to see Chip lying there on his back. He was fast asleep, with a pistol that Mama had given him clutched in his hand, which lay across his breast.

It was an unwritten rule in Vicksburg: People did not give their nigras guns. But somehow, in the face of the siege and living in caves and Pa being gone and everything being turned upside down, the rules didn't stand anymore. So Mama had given Chip a revolver. She and I both had been surprised to see that he knew how to use it.

He'd told Mama yesterday, "Nobody gonna get in this cave, not while I gots breath left in my body."

I stepped over him carefully and Sammy jumped over him lightly. And then I picked Sammy up, and taking the same path as Pa and I had taken, we entered the woods and headed down toward the stream.

And then I saw that something else was going on, something more that qualified under rules that didn't stand anymore. I would not have believed it if I had not seen it with my own eyes. Something I knew I could tell my grandchildren about someday, the way my grandmother told me stories about when she went to school in Paris in 1826.

Camped hard by the stream was the 1st Missouri Brigade. Yankees. And visiting with them were one or two members of the 3rd Louisiana Confederates.

They were *visiting*. Like a town meeting at home!

I heard laughter. I heard something about borrowed coffee made of sweet potatoes. And the weather. Then more laughter. Then the word *Rebs*.

I clutched Sammy to me and hurried on.

I finally reached the spot in the stream where it curved and where Pa and I used to pick blackberries. It was so quiet and peaceful here. The birds sang as if there weren't any fool war. I smelled jasmine, honeysuckle, and apricots. I put Sammy down and he rubbed against my ankles. I set about picking the blackberries.

Ridiculous soldiers, I thought. Visiting back and forth and making jokes when all night long they were doing their best to blow each other's heads off. And look at what they'd done to us. Our beautiful town looked like something the giant in *Jack in the Beanstalk* had wreaked his havoc on. Houses were shattered, gardens ruined, people and animals killed, a whole way of life ruined.

The two-quart pail was near filled with blackberries when I heard voices carried on the clear morning air.

"I tell you, I have to put a bandage on it. And some laudanum. I can sprinkle the laudanum on. It'll help ease the pain."

There were certain inflections in the voice that reminded me of Pa. And it was a doctor talking. Could Pa be back, without telling us? I picked the pail up with one hand and Sammy with the other. "Who do you think it is?" I asked him.

He purred his "I don't know."

Half bravely, I followed the stream around its bend, and there found two soldiers. One was seated on a rock beside the stream. He was definitely Confederate.

The other had his back to me. But even then I knew he was Yankee because of the blue coat. And an officer because of the trappings on his uniform.

And a doctor because of the yellow hospital flag he'd stuck in the horse's reins. Pa had told me about that flag and how it was respected when a doctor soldier from an opposing side went through enemy lines.

This wasn't Pa, though, because there was no gray in his hair. Landon? Yes, I recognized the spread of his shoulders. His horse, Rosie.

The Confederate wore no shirt, and Landon was bandaging his shoulder, expertly. There was blood on the Confederate's arm. It was he who sighted me first. He cleared his throat and whispered something to his blue-coated friend.

I calculated a little humor wouldn't hurt about now. "More visiting," I said in contempt. "You people make me sick. You kill each other all night long and in the morning you visit and drink coffee and fix each other's hurts. What about what you've done to our town? To our people?"

Landon stood up straight but did not turn around. "There can be only one person on God's earth who would say such a thing," he said. "My sister, Claire Louise."

And then he turned around.

He looked so tall in his uniform. And it was kind of

dusty, and the top buttons of the coat were not closed. His face was sunburned, a wide-brimmed hat was set aside with his sword. He wore his sidearm. "Hello, Claire Louise," he said.

"Hello, Landon. What are you doing here?"

"I might ask the same of you. You've got black and blue all over you, so you must have been picking berries, and if you've eaten too many, it means I'll have to give you some kind of a decoction later on. You've got a cat in your arms and the hem of your dress and your shoes are soaking wet. Which translates into a sore throat. Your face has high color. Do you have a fever?"

"You have one patient already. Isn't that enough?"

He grinned. God, that grin could break your heart. That old crooked grin that made all the girls swoon.

"You need a shave," I told him. I liked the way he looked with a couple of days' worth of dark beard on his face. Like a villain in an English novel.

Behind him, his friend was painfully reaching for his shirt, embarrassed at being seen without one by a girl. If he'd known all the times I'd seen Landon without one, he wouldn't care.

"I know. I was going to shave after I fixed up Robert here. By the way, this is my friend, Robert, whom I've known for weeks and wasn't firing upon yesterday. May I remind you that I don't kill people? Robert, this is my little sister, Claire Louise. Sweet child if you can take the mouth she gives you."

"I'm not a child anymore," I told him. "I'm thir-teen now."

He looked at me from beneath lowered eyelids, while he straightened things in his medical bag. He was trying to figure what I was saying.

"Since when?" he asked.

"Since last June."

"Well then, you're a proper young lady. Congratula-tions. See that you act it."

I stuck my tongue out at him.

He sighed. "I meant around boys," he said.

Was he going to give me that lecture, too? How to act around boys now that I had my woman's time of the month? I'd gotten this talk from Pa, from Mama, from Easter and Clothilda, from everybody except James and Sammy, the cat.

He gave the subject a new turn. "We're headed to Jackson. Robert's family lives there."

I gasped. "You mean you're not coming home?"

He sobered. "Am I wanted?"

"Landon Corbet, you haven't got the sense of a wet otter," I scolded him. "Mama's been praying for you. And praying you'd come home. She'd just faint away if I told her you were here and didn't. You've got to come. We live in a cave, yes, like everybody else. But it's big, and we've got all the conveniences of home. And we've got room for you both. Now you just mind me and come."

He looked at Robert. "Doesn't it appear to you that I'm the one who's supposed to be doing the scolding here?"

Robert remained neutral. But it was more than that. He just didn't smile. He hadn't yet, not with his mouth or his eyes, and I supposed he had a beautiful smile.

He must be carrying around a fearful burden, I told myself. I wondered if Landon knows about it.

"I'll wager a month's pay my mama doesn't know where she is right now," Landon was saying to Robert. Well?" He looked at me. "Does she?"

"No," I admitted shamefacedly.

"So with all she's got to worry about, you're giving her more."

I put down Sammy and the blackberries. "Landon, can I hug you?"

"Oh no you don't. Playing on my sympathies. And you're about as helpless as a Yankee in a bayonet charge." But he took me in his arms anyway, and his hug was like coming home for me. When I was in need of a hug from Pa, and Pa held off for some reason he was using to play on my senses, Landon always supplied it. And he always knew the right moment, too.

"Hello, Claire Louise," he said gently. "Are you still my little orphan girl?"

"Landon, I'll soon be fourteen."

Then he touched my forehead. "You do have a fever, sweetie." He got serious. "What's wrong? Something bad happen? Come on. Up here on Rosie with me." He lifted me onto his horse. "You fill me in on the way home."

He tied on my pail of blackberries, and put Sammy in

an empty saddlebag with just his head sticking out. Robert got atop his horse, too.

"We'd best get home before the shelling starts again," he said.

We rode ahead, and Robert followed at a discreet distance. We walked the horses slowly and carefully. Landon found himself saluted several times, even though he was in enemy territory.

"These Southerners are nothing if not polite," he said, joking about himself. "So"—he poked me in the ribs—"what's happened to make you so upset?"

So I told him. About losing Jewel and Diamond.

"That's considerable bad," he agreed.

I told him about Sarah running off to join the Confederate army as a man. He was taken, even more, with that. "Damned stubborn girl," he swore. "Excuse my language, Claire Louise. Why'd she go and do a thing like that?"

"You won't scold if I tell you?"

"Tell me."

"She did it to worry you. That's what she said, anyway. To punish you."

"Who'd she join up with?"

"She didn't say. Just said she was going to be with Lee in the Cumberland Valley."

"That's where Pa is. I'll write to him and tell him to be on the lookout."

We rode in silence for a moment. It seemed like I

could feel the confusion, the anger, and the anguish coming off his very being.

"She won't get far," he finally said. "First time she gets scraped by a minie ball, the doctor will find out she's a girl and she'll be sent home."

"Would you tell on her?" I asked.

"Don't know," he said gruffly. "Do know that she wouldn't have run off if I'd been home."

"What would you have done?"

"Would have spanked her good first, and then married her. She needs both."

"Landon, you're really besotted with her. I think she is with you, too."

Another poke in the ribs. "Mind yourself."

"Do I get a question now?"

"Yes. One."

"Landon," I asked softly, "what's wrong with Robert?"

"Took a minie ball in the shoulder at the Big Black River."

I knew he was lying.

"But why is he so . . ."

"So what?"

"Like he's carrying such a burden inside him?"

"You mean suspicious, mistrusting, and fearful?"

"Yes."

"He's no coward. Let's get that straight now. He does have a burden. But I can't tell what it is. Patient-doctor relationship."

"Oh, Landon."

One more poke, this one harder. "That's all. No more questions. My God, look at those caves on that hillside. What in the name of all that's holy have they done to my Vicksburg?"

I got defensive. "If not for the caves, we'd all be dead," I told him.

He turned in the saddle and spoke to Robert. "Let me apologize for my town, Robert," he said. "But this is what you get for being the only rail and river junction between here and Memphis and New Orleans."

"It can be made right again," Robert said wisely. Apparently, to him, anything that could be made right again was not worth wasting your time worrying about. There were things that never could be made right again, he was reminding my brother.

Landon sighed. "Come on, Claire Louise, show us the right cave," he directed.

CHAPTER SIX

MAMA STARED at me across what was now her dining area. I handed Sammy to James, whose face was swollen with crying. He held the cat close and made a gulping ending to the crying he'd been doing all morning, thinking the cat was gone for good.

"He wouldn't eat breakfast, he wouldn't listen to any reasoning," Mama told me. "I tell you, I couldn't bear it. And now he's running a fever and hiccuping. You know what his hiccups are like. Just like Claire Louise's. They last *hours*. To say nothing of the worry I had over *you*, Claire Louise. I tell you, I wish I'd left you with your grandmother."

"I have somebody outside who can fix James up," I said softly.

"I don't know why I didn't leave you there. Your father has a fixation about the family being together, is why. And I don't know why I just don't take up a wooden spoon and paddle you good right now. What did you say? You brought someone home? Into this quagmire? Who?"

He'd sneaked in behind me. "It's me, Mama," Landon

said. He came right past me, putting a reassuring hand on my shoulder, and went directly into Mama's arms.

"Oh, my boy, my boy." She clung to him, crying. He was at least two heads taller than she was.

"It's all right," he kept saying, "I'm home. I'm here. I'm fine, Mama. All in one piece." He lifted her right off the floor and held her. She reached for her handkerchief and blotted her tears.

"God is good," she said.

"Yeah," Landon said, "though sometimes He gets a little confused. Having trouble with the kids are you, Mama?" He released her and leaned down next to James, who sat with the cat in his arms. "How you doin', Buddy?"

James smiled at him. A knowing and secretive smile. They hugged, Sammy squashed between them. They had a great deal of feeling for each other, these two. James worshipped Landon and Landon didn't treat him like a child. He talked to him like a man, and James responded in kind.

Landon felt his face. "You seem a bit warm, Buddy. You know, I got the greatest new fixings for fever. You take some of it, and I'll take you outside to give some carrots to Rosie before the shelling starts again. What do you say?"

James said yes.

Landon stood and took James by the hand and they went toward the hall. "My bag is outside," he said. "Hope you got carrots, Ma." And then, "I'm bringing somebody else back in. Hope you got coffee, too. Oh, and I don't mean to outrank you, Ma, but she's too big for paddlin'. I'll talk to her if you want. Just let me know."

He winked at me and tweaked my nose as they walked out into the sunlight.

Within less than an hour, Robert was welcomed, sat down at the table, plied with food, fussed over by Mama, undressed, and washed by Easter, who told him to hush his mouth. She worked, even now, at the hospital two days a week and if she hadn't seen it already, then it didn't exist.

They gave him a room of his own with clean sheets and a light summer blanket. Easter approved Landon's bandaging of Robert and told him to go and clean up, too, or did he want *her* to do it. After all, "it ain't been that long since I done it when you wuz a little boy, Master Landon."

Landon skedaddled out of there, quick as he could.

But not before he took me into my room, where he put a newfangled thing called a thermometer into my mouth. When he took it out, he showed me my temperature. "One hundred and two," he said.

Then he gave me a dose of quinine and told me to get out of my wet shoes and stockings and dress and go to bed. I put on my nightgown and followed him into the kitchen.

He'd already dosed James with medicine, he told Mama, and Easter had put him to bed. With the cat.

"What is the fever from?" Mama asked. "This place is clean. I wouldn't have moved here if it weren't."

"Change of climate," he told her. "Undo excitement

over being shelled. Something in the water supply. Or something in the sand itself that surrounds you. I wouldn't stay here a minute more than I had to, Ma. The kids'll be all right for now, though, I promise. And I'm on leave. If worse comes to worse, I can get them back to our grandparents, if you want."

"I don't want to go," I put in. "I want to stay here with you, Mama."

"You still here?" Landon looked up. The look was severe. "Go and do as you're told."

I went, but I lingered outside the kitchen, listening. "I'd wager half the people in these caves have it," he was saying. "And they don't even know it." Then another turn in conversation. "Ma, did you know that Sarah went and joined the army as a man?"

"No!" Mama was taken aback. "All I know is that she came to your father one day and had him remove the mole on her face so she wouldn't be recognized. Oh, Landon, I'm so sorry."

"I should have married her when I had the chance," he said.

"Would that have changed things?"

"Yes. I think she did it to get back at me. Because I wanted to wait until after the war was over. Look, when she sees what it's like out there, she'll be back. She won't be able to take it."

Silence for a moment. Then Mama asked, "Tell me about Robert, Landon."

He shrugged. "Can't, Ma. He's got trouble. Big as a panther in a hen house. But I can't tell. Doctor-patient relationship."

"Oh, you sound just like your father."

He sighed deeply. "I guess we all sound the same after a while."

He was saying something about going to the surgery when the shelling stopped.

I ran to my room down the hall. I sat on the bed. I suppose it was the quinine, but soon I was fast asleep.

"YOU ALL must have a fearful number of dogs in this town," Robert said at breakfast the next morning.

"What makes you say that?" Mama asked.

"'Cause every time a shell bursts the dogs all send up a god-awful howl. Seems they're the only ones who have any sense."

"Did they keep you awake last night?" Mama pushed.

"No, ma'am. I got plenty else to keep me awake."

He was a handsome man, now that I had a chance to really take his measure. His serious manner gave him an appearance of dignity as much as the mustache and goatee he wore. I imagined the piercing blue eyes could smile if they chose to.

"Claire Louise, eat your breakfast if you want to come back to the house with me later," Landon said quietly.

I gasped. "Can I?" I looked at Mama. "Mama, can I?"

"If you eat and mind yourself," she said. "It'll be a

good chance for you and Landon to catch up with each other. Sometimes I think what you need around here, Claire Louise, is your older brother to keep you in line."

Landon grinned. I stuck my tongue out at him. "I'd go along, but I'm sorry to say I'm too weak to make the trip," Robert apologized.

"You are going back to bed," Landon told him firmly, "until I figure out just what kind of fever you have. It's not like the children's, that I know. Ma, which hospital do you help out with on occasion? The one for the really wounded who need amputations? Or the one for the sick who can go back to serve?"

"The badly wounded," she said. "That's where Dr. Balfour is."

"I'd like to see him this morning."

"Oh, good. Here, let me pen him a note and invite him to tea someday. We mustn't stop being civilized just because we live in a cave."

She laughed at her own joke, Mama did, as she went over to her ladies' desk in the corner and wrote the note. Before she had finished, the shelling stopped. We all knew it meant the Yankee artillery were taking time for breakfast. Eight o'clock.

"I don't know when we'll be back," Landon said. He kissed Mama on the cheek. "We may have to stay until the noon cease-fire. If that happens, don't worry. C'mon, Claire Louise. Robert, get back to bed. James, mind Ma."

"Why can't I go?" James put in. "Sammy will be good."

"You and Sammy take a walk with Ma now. You've got near an hour. And don't be a pest to Robert."

Soon as we started walking away from the cave, people began coming out of their "rat holes," as they were beginning to call them, for some air. We couldn't walk very far before they spotted Landon, came up to him, shook his hand, and asked him what Grant intended to do. "Do you think he'll take the town, Dr. Corbet?" came the question.

And, "Do you know where your pa is?"

And, "How's your mama? Give her our best."

And, "You seeing patients in your pa's surgery at all?"

Landon was polite and courteous to all of them. The Yankee uniform mattered not a bit. Folks considered him one of their own.

"How is the food holding out, Claire Louise? Tell me what you know about it."

"We brought with us a half barrel of flour and sugar each," I told him, "same with cornmeal, three sides of bacon, two smoked hams, some containers of coffee and tea, sugar, and eggs. About every other day Andy sends down two quarts of milk from Buttercup, the cow from home. We have enough."

"When I told Mr. Bullock before that I didn't know what Grant was intending, I was lying, Claire Louise. He intends to take Vicksburg. The devils all left hell, you see, and they're here. You all are going to live in that cave a long time. Grant doesn't know the meaning of the word 'lose.' And the people in this town are too god-awful proud to surrender."

I did not answer. I did not quite understand, though I sensed something terrible in his voice.

"I'm thinking, the Rebs must have army stores. One of these days Robert is going to do us a good turn. Dress up in his uniform and secure us some provisions. He just can't make his presence known right now. He has to stay secluded."

"Why?"

He gave a deep sigh. "Because he's a wanted man by his own army. If he's caught, they'll shoot him. That's all I can say right now. Don't ask me anything else."

He gave me the small yellow flag to carry. We walked in silence for a minute. It was more than silence on my part. I was struck dumb.

"Don't tell Ma any of this," he said.

I promised I wouldn't. What had Robert done? No wonder his eyes looked haunted, like he knew every sin of the world. I looked at my brother as we walked up a hill and toward a tented hospital, and I wondered how he could keep the secrets of so many people and not burst like a Parrott shell inside.

CHAPTER SEVEN

LANDON EXPLAINED to me about the Confederate hospital system, and then about how Pa and Dr. Balfour went way back and how I must always respect Dr. Balfour because he was the most esteemed physician for miles around.

"Even more than Pa?" I asked.

"Not as far as we're concerned," he joked. He pulled my hair on the side where it fell to my shoulders. He looked at me long and meaningful, as if he hadn't seen me in a long time, which he hadn't, if you discount the last visit home, which had been so fast we scarcely had time to say hello.

"You're growing up," he said, as if surprised.

"I keep trying to tell people that."

"You're getting so darned pretty it scares me. I meant it when I said yesterday that you'd better start behaving yourself around boys."

"Pa won't let me see any boys. Ma, neither. Not alone, anyways." I blinked my lashes at him. "Do you suppose you can take my side on that when the argument comes up?"

"Shouldn't be any argument. You behave yourself and start acting like a young lady and I'll talk to them about it when I get the chance."

"Oh, thank you, Landon. They always listen to you." Impulsively, I hugged him, right there in the street.

"Hey," he said, looking around, somewhat embarrassed. "I have to behave myself in public, too, you know."

But he smiled and we kept walking. "I need to talk to Balfour," he said. "Will you be all right in the hospital?"

I nodded.

"Look, maybe I shouldn't have brought you along. You sure? Some women swoon. Some cry. You won't embarrass me like that, will you?"

I said no, I wouldn't. Even though I didn't know. I was still busy being amazed that Landon could walk through the streets and not be arrested in his Yankee uniform. Or even approached and asked to explain himself. Even with the yellow flag.

"Because of his profession he'll be allowed to go anywhere," Mama had said.

People assumed he was on an important mission. As he was, this morning. After all, he was honor bound to treat anyone who was hurt. He'd already told me he'd treated Confederates in his Federal hospital tent, hadn't he? Wasn't he treating Robert?

"A captain from the 3rd Louisiana I met recently," he was saying, "told me that the hospital population in this town is eight hundred. I think it's more."

I was so proud of my brother! So proud that he could fix people, save them from dying, and the minute we went inside the first hospital tent I knew there would be no question of his being a Yankee. The tent was large and filled with rows and rows of cots on which lay our "brave boys," as Mama called them. At the end of one row of cots was a doctor wearing an apron stained with blood, as if he had just rewrapped a wound. He was aided by a nigra nurse.

All stared at us as we came in. Hands of those on the cot were raised in supplication. One or two of the bodies said, "Water, water." Others said, "Over here, Doc, I need some morphine, please."

Another addressed me, "You a nuss, miss? All I need is someone to write to my mama for me. I think I'm dying."

I backed up a little behind Landon. "You all right?" he asked.

"Yes."

"It's the first five minutes that gets you. Concentrate on the smell of lavender and cologne. Here." He drew Mama's note out of his tunic pocket and gave it to me. "When I tell you to go and give it to Dr. Balfour, go."

We waited a few moments, while the doctor had a patient carefully lifted from the table where he was being treated to his bed. "He's in blue heaven from the chloroform," he told them, "but that doesn't mean you can throw him around. Be careful with him."

"Go now, while he's between patients," Landon said.

I covered the small distance between Dr. Balfour and us in a few strides. He was wiping his face with a rag. He looked at me. "Claire Louise, what is it? Everything all right at your house? Here, what have you got, a note from your mother? Sashee," he said to the nigra nurse, "I think I'll take a few minutes. Clean up the table and get me a fresh basin of hot water and soap." He read the note in a second and looked beyond me and extended his hand. "You don't need any introduction, son," he said to Landon. "I've known you since you were knee-high."

The two of them embraced.

"So," Dr. Balfour said, "your father told me you went and joined the Yanks. Tore him up quite a bit, it did, in the beginning, didn't it?"

"Yes, sir," Landon answered.

Dr. Balfour found three chairs in a corner and gestured we should sit. "So how's business with the Yankees these days?"

"I think you hold the record for cutting off a leg in three minutes," Landon said, "anyways, that's what Pa told me."

"You didn't take your life in your hands and cross Confederate lines to congratulate me on that, did you, Captain?"

"No, sir," Landon blushed.

But Dr. Balfour knew. "Claire Louise," he said, "you

know that young soldier who asked you to write a letter home for him before?"

"Yessir."

"Well, if Sashee here gives you pen and paper, how about you do it for him?"

I was shocked. I never would have thought of it. "Can I?" I asked Landon.

"I think it'd be a good idea," he said softly.

So I went with Sashee, the slim young colored girl, who took me through the lines of cots and found me a chair.

Before I sat down, I looked back at Landon and the doctor. Landon was leaning over in his chair, his elbows on his knees, as if he was confiding in Dr. Balfour. The doctor was listening intently.

And I knew, in those places in your bones where you know such things, that Landon was telling Balfour about Robert. And asking advice about him. It was that serious. Landon was up a tree right now and his conscience was throwing stones at him and he had to figure out how to get down because the tree was soon going to be cut into pieces.

With him in it.

"Claire Louise, this is Bobby Joe," Sashee said.

We said hello.

He was young, not more than sixteen. He had only one leg, the other long since taken off, and he was here now for his right arm, which had been hit by a minie ball.

He was handsome with thick curly brown hair, blue eyes, and a freckled face. "I got to write to my mama," he said. "She must know I'm still livin' though I may not be alive much longer. Will you take down my words?"

I said I would, and I did.

His words were polite and concerned. He inquired about everyone in his family. He came from a farm family in Tennessee and he apologized for not being able to carry his weight when he made it home.

"Mama," he said, "I think that on Judgment Day there's gonna be such a scramblin' for arms and legs as you never did see. Why, look at me alone. I'll have to go to Antietam to get my leg, then back here to Vicksburg for my arm. 'Cause the doctor ain't seen it yet this mornin', Mama, but it's all swollen and red and I'll likely have to be shed of it. The Lord'll just have to have patience with me."

I could scarce see the finishing lines for my tears, which I fought to keep back. And I kissed his forehead when I said good-bye. "You'll make it, Bobby Joe," I said as I left him there.

Landon and I both had our spirits on the floor when we left the hospital. Neither one of us asked the other why. I suppose it's why we get along so well. We respect each other's feelings.

CHAPTER EIGHT

WE STOPPED at our house on the way home, joyous to find it had not yet been shelled or destroyed in any way. Landon said he thought Mama ought to offer it for a residence hospital, that he'd talk to her about it.

Andy and Clothilda were there, and since the shelling had commenced Landon said we should go into the cellar to wait it out.

"No," I said, "not the cellar."

He had taken a letter out of his pocket. I'd seen Dr. Balfour give it to him, heard him say that the Confederate dispatch rider had been through this morning, asking him to find Dr. Corbet. Landon was reading the soiled and wrinkled envelope, not looking at me.

"What do you mean 'not the cellar'?"

"I'm afraid of the cellar."

He sighed, stuffed the envelope back in his coat pocket, and gave me his full attention. "You mean you still haven't gotten over that nonsense?"

I blushed. "No."

"Well, maybe a day and a night down there would cure you of it then."

I bit my bottom lip. "Please, Landon."

He took pity on me. His voice went kind. "Look, I'll go with you. We'll stay until the shelling stops. I'll have Clothilda bring us some food, and I promise I won't leave you. How's that?"

I said all right. Hesitantly. I followed him down, trying to ignore the shadows and the dark corners that had so terrorized my childhood. As soon as we had found some old blankets and settled on the floor, Landon opened and reread the letter.

Shells burst outside, Porter's shells from the river.

"I've been reassigned," Landon said. "To the division hospital at Milliken's Bend, close by. Grant wants to make it a hospital for the slightly injured who can be made well quickly so they can go back into the field as replacements. The Sanitary Commission has brought three boats of supplies and doctors and nurses down the river to get started. I report by the beginning of July."

He looked at me. "At least I won't be far from home. I can still keep an eye on you," he teased, but I sensed there was some sadness in his demeanor. And then I thought of something.

"What of Robert?" I said.

He shrugged, and looked terrible sad. "I have to figure out what to do with him before then," he said quietly. "Just make up my mind and do it."

"Landon, I don't understand. Isn't it Robert's place to decide what to do? I mean, is he your prisoner or something?"

"You're too wise for your age, you know that?"

I pouted. The shells were exploding overhead regularly now. One was especially loud and close and I ducked, instinctively. Just then Andy came down the steps and sought Landon out.

"Mister Landon. Suh?"

"Yes, Andy, over here."

He had two pillows and two blankets in one arm and a basket of fried chicken and biscuits in the other. "Clothilda, she say you all shud eat, then catch some shut-eye if 'n you can wif those shells screamin' out there. They won't stop till noon."

"Thank you, Andy." Landon took the pillows and blankets and threw one of each at me. "Clothilda's orders," he said. "Here, take some food. And then get some sleep."

"Mister Landon, suh?" Andy was still standing there, shifting his weight from one foot to the other. "I gots a favor to axe you."

"Have at it, Andy."

"Well, the other day when I wuz washin' Mr. Robert he wuz tellin' me how he wants to go home. Only he gots no money to travel. I wuz thinkin', suh, if 'n it be okay wif you an' your mama, if 'n I hire myself out to dig a cave. There's a gentleman I know who will pay up to fifty dollars to get himself a cave dug proper like. I could do it in my spare time and give the money to Robert, suh. If'n it be okay wif you."

Landon was silent for a moment, taking it in. "Confederate money?" he asked. "Or Yankee dollars?"

"Why, Confederate, I 'spect," Andy told him.

Landon sighed. "Confederate paper is sixty cents to the Yankee dollar, but it's still sound," Landon said. "If you're willing to do it, Andy, go right ahead. I'll clear it with my mother. Now I have a favor to ask you."

"Yessuh."

"I'm dying for a cup of coffee, Andy."

"Bring it right quick, suh."

"Me, too?" I begged. "Please, Landon, Ma lets me have it."

He said all right and Andy went back upstairs to fetch it.

That coffee was wonderful, hot and sweet, and I must admit that the fried chicken and biscuits tasted like angel food. We ate in pleasant comradeship. Then I settled myself under my blanket and closed my eyes.

"You still awake?" Landon asked.

"Yes."

"You hear that from Andy? It means Robert is planning on going home."

"Well, what else did you think he was planning on?"

He closed his eyes for a minute, like he was praying. "Claire Louise, sit up. I have to talk to you," he said.

"Landon," I whined, "five minutes ago you told me to go to sleep. And now you tell me—"

"Claire Louise, shut your mouth and listen to me!"

I sat up. "Not if you talk to me like that, I won't."

He sighed heavily. He gathered himself in. "I'm sorry," he said. "I'm sorry, but I need somebody to listen. I just got done talking to Dr. Balfour about Robert, and he gave me his professional physician's opinion of what I *had* to do to save my army career and my reputation as a doctor. As well as my family name. I know he's right, but I still can't bear to think about it. I've become friends with Robert. Did you hear that? I don't even know his last name. He won't tell me, and yet I've become friends with him. And now, if I listen to Balfour, and my own conscience, I have to turn him in."

I listened, respectfully. He was going on like he would never stop. Like somebody had loosened something in him. He was pouring out his heart. To me.

"What did he do?" I whispered.

"Do? Yes, there is that, too, isn't there. As well as the fact that he deserted. All right, I'm going to tell you, Claire Louise. But you must swear to me that you'll never tell another soul."

I swore. He nodded his head, accepting my word. And then he told me.

"Do you remember the battle of Antietam? Last fall?"

"Yes. We lost it."

"Well, Robert is the reason the South lost it."

I looked at him as if he'd taken leave of his senses.

"Did you ever hear of Lee's lost Order Number 191?"
I searched my memory. "I recollect Pa talking about it.
Reading about it in the *Citizen*."

"Last September ninth Lee wrote an order," he explained. "In it were the details of the march of his army,
which had all but disappeared behind the Blue Ridge
Mountains during its invasion of the North. The Yankees
never knew where he was. And Bobby Lee wanted the orders to be circulated to his division commanders. They
were given out to staff officers to be delivered to those
commanders.

"One of those officers was Robert. He told Lee his
courier delivered the order to Hill. But to his disgrace, if
you will, Hill never signed for it. Robert had no signature.

"Nobody did. The order was lost. Four days later it
was in Union hands."

I gasped. "How did it get there?"

"Good question. The Confederate bigwigs are still in-
vestigating. All they know is that the order was found by
a private named Mitchell of the 27th Indiana in an envelope containing three cigars wrapped in a piece of paper.
The piece of paper was the orders. The 27th Indiana was
encamped on a former Confederate campground."

I found myself shaking. I drew my blanket closer.
"But what of Robert?"

"He told me that piece of paper dropped out of his
pocket before he could give it to his courier. This takes his

courier off the hook because Hill never signed for the order. It all goes back to Robert, but they can't prove anything. But it's the result of it all that matters.

"Lincoln's General McCellan was able to make an immediate strike at Lee's army because of the intelligence he got from that piece of paper. Four days later we had the battle of Antietam because of it. England pulled back on any promises of aid to the South because of the loss at Antietam. And I have on my hands a severely depressed and confused and guilty Robert because of it. And that's why Dr. Balfour says I should turn him in."

Silence between us then. My head whirred. "And what will you do?"

"I don't know, Claire Louise. I have a week to have a crisis of conscience. I want to aid him in getting home. I know I should walk over to brigade headquarters this day and tell General Pemberton that I have him. Either way I'm in hell."

I crawled out from under my blanket and over to him and gave him a hug. "I'll help you, whatever you do," I said.

He hugged me back. "I can't drag my family into this. When I met him, he was a wounded Confederate soldier who'd fought in a minor skirmish to do something decent. I was honor bound to do something for him. I'm still not sure he won't lose that arm."

He released me. "Hey, the shelling's stopped. It must be noon. Let's get home," he said.

I giggled.

"What's so funny?"

"You said home. And we are home," I told him. "I want to go upstairs and get a pillowcase full of clean clothes for me and Mama. Can I?"

He said yes. He also said he wanted to give me something. So he came upstairs and while I gathered clothes for myself and Mama and James, he stuffed his whole set of Dickens into a pillowcase. As well as some of his childhood books, for James.

"For you to read," he said of the Dickens, "during those terrible times when the shells are falling. These books will get you through. I promise."

CHAPTER NINE

WHEN WE got home that afternoon, things were in chaos. No, the shelling hadn't started again, not yet, but Mama was at the dining table, seated across from James, and both were crying.

Easter stood by, near tears herself, and Robert was in back of Easter, unable to stand on his own two feet but holding onto a kitchen cupboard and trying to soothe the lot of them.

"I can take care of it, ma'am," he was saying to Mama.

"No, no, Robert. Landon said I was not to allow you out of the house."

"But a snake on the roof!" Robert was saying.

I followed Landon in. He set down his pillowcase of books. "Who's got a snake on the roof?" he asked. "Ma? What's wrong? Why are you crying? James? Did you get hurt?"

James would not look at him.

"Well, somebody tell me what's going on here," Landon said irritably. "It can't be as bad as what's going on out there."

"There's a snake on one of the posts of the roof," Robert told him. "I wanted to go out and kill it, but your mother here won't allow me outside. Says she's going according to your orders."

"She is. You can scarce stand," Landon said. "How can you battle a snake?"

"It isn't only that," Robert reported. "It seems that your little brother here has been playing with your matches and started a small fire."

Sure enough, there on the table were the remnants of a small fire. The day's copy of the *Daily Citizen,* which was the only newspaper now being printed in Vicksburg, and printed on the back of old wallpaper at that, was singed around the edges. It looked as if it had been on fire and then that fire hastily put out. Around it were several of Landon's large glue and phosphorous matches, which I knew he had cautioned James never to touch.

Landon took it all in. He stepped forward, closer to James, who was still sobbing quietly. "You did this, did you?" His voice was stern, not kind.

"I didn't . . . mean . . . to." James hiccuped.

"What do you mean you didn't mean to?" Landon asked.

James didn't answer. He kept his eyes downcast. This was not his Landon talking to him now, this was someone else, someone who frightened him.

"Look," Landon said, "I think you better go into your room and sit there and think on what you've done. And

I'll be in later and we'll talk about it. You hear? Go on, now."

James didn't move. "But I wanted . . . I wanted to see you kill the snake," he all but wailed.

In an instant Landon picked James up off the chair, set him firmly on the ground, and gave him a small spank on the bottom and a shove toward the hall. "Go and do as I say," he ordered.

James ran. Landon then walked Robert back to his room, and they were in there a few minutes. I heard low talking. I supposed Robert had his fever again. But when Landon came back out into the kitchen he said nothing about Robert. All he said was, "Stop crying, Mama, everything will be all right."

"No, there's more, Landon, there's more."

"All right, have at it. Might as well, Mama."

"Well, you know how I give Easter five dollars and send her to market every morning to see what she can find in the way of meat?"

"If you're going to tell me there isn't any more meat in the marketplace, Mama, I've already been apprised of that fact. Clothilda, at home, wants permission to kill the last turkey. Says it's old and it's tough, but at least it's not mule meat. Can I tell her yes?"

Mama nodded, blowing her nose and wiping her eyes. Landon leaned over her, pushing back the strands of blonde hair that had escaped from her rolled-back hairdo. "C'mon, Ma," he said, "I need some moral support, too."

"Easter saw that they had not only mule meat hanging there, but rats," Mama said. "Oh, Landon, what's my town come to?"

He sighed and said nothing. "Did you get a letter from Pa today?"

"No. The Confederate dispatch rider came through but there was nothing from your pa. Only this, from Dr. Balfour." She gave him one piece of paper on which was scrawled a note. He read it carefully and handed it to me.

"Ma and I will discuss it," he told me, "but you ought to have a say in it, since it concerns you. Think about it and let me know tomorrow."

I took the note and scanned it quickly. Dr. Balfour was asking my mother's and Landon's permission to allow me to come to the hospital twice a week and write letters home for the brave boys who needed them written. I was good at the task, Dr. Balfour wrote, and sympathetic with the young men without being disheartening.

I looked up from my reading. They were both eyeing me.

"Don't do it if you don't want to," Mama advised.

"Being around the sick and dying can steal your soul right from under you," Landon said.

I nodded and said nothing. Landon told Easter there was still some time before the shelling started, and anyway he knew the nigras knew their way around town so's they wouldn't get hit, so could she please go to our home and tell Clothilda to kill that turkey and bring it home so Easter could cook it for supper?

Easter left.

"Now," Landon said, "let's go and kill ourselves a snake."

It was wrapped around the upright roof support post, and by now a small crowd had gathered. Landon urged them back a ways in case it attacked, for it was surely poisonous. Then he unsheathed his sword and with that terrible and beautiful instrument poked at the head of the snake to annoy it. Behind us the crowd *ooh*ed and *aah*ed.

It was very fat must have been very long because it had itself wrapped around that support post at least four or five times.

Now it was watching Landon, fastening its yellow-green eyes upon him, opening its devil's mouth so its tongue could flicker in and out. Landon did more poking with that sword of his and, angry at being disturbed, the snake fought back. It unwrapped itself two or three turns from that support post and slithered down the roof of the cave toward Landon.

Everyone gave a low moan.

Then Landon went at it. The snake responded with back-and-forth thrusts of about two feet of itself, finally got tired, lost balance, and slipped to the earth at Landon's feet.

Quick as a firefly, Landon thrust his sword and cut its head off. I thought I was going to throw up. The snake was still moving. Now *I* was crying.

A man, a fellow cave dweller, came up to Landon, waited for him to sheath his sword, and shook his hand.

"I'm Oldfield from down ways a bit. Glad you're with us. All these people knew what to do, but they wanted to see their own major in action."

"Won't be with you all long," Landon addressed them quietly, "so I'd suggest you all learn to do it yourselves. And I'm not a major. Just a captain. If you see another snake just keep the people away from it and go and fetch one of your soldiers I see wandering about. You'll be all right."

Back in the cave he told Mama how he'd been reassigned to the hospital at Milliken's Bend and how, this afternoon, he wanted to take a ride down there to introduce himself to his commanding officer before he reported for duty. He'd be in late, he told her. We were to keep an eye on Robert. "Give him some more quinine if his fever persists."

First, though, he had to clean himself up, polish his boots, and walk home to get Rosie, his horse. And he had to talk with James.

"Your father would paddle him good," Mama said.

I followed him down the hall. "Landon."

"Yes?"

"Pa wouldn't. He wouldn't paddle James. He never hit us."

His smile now was solemn. "I know, Claire Louise. I was once a little boy in this family, too, remember? Now don't worry yourself. I know what I'm about."

CHAPTER TEN

I THINK it is eighteen days now that we have lived in our cave.

I never thought I could learn to do this. I, who come from a bedroom with English wallpaper and Persian rugs.

I never thought I would see my mother do it. But she does. She has accommodated herself, like Lady Jane Grey did when she was sent to the Tower of London. That is how I see her when I come into the kitchen mornings, after we have spent the night with the thundering of the Parrott guns, the unrelenting fire of small arms, the shrill whistling of shells. Early this morning, though, what woke me was the cooing of swallows on our roof.

I found Mama at the table, dressed in her morning gown, sipping her tea, just as she'd be in her sun-filled dining room at home. Never mind that she is worried about the shortage of food, or if the mail will come through.

Does she think, even for a moment, of the pots of flowers she left on the front steps at home? Does she wonder if our house will be hit with cannon fire this day?

I do, though I do not mention such to her. I just sit down at the table with her and pour myself some tea.

But there is one good thing we have working in our favor. Unlike a lot of other caves around us, we have water. Pa made sure of that. Unfortunate others trudge, daily, with pails and buckets to the stream far below us to fetch water of an uncertain color and character, to wash with, cook with, and even drink. As at home, we have a cistern in the cellar of this cave, round and full of God's good rainwater. And we all, in turn, go down with a lantern and becalm ourselves and bathe with some of Mama's lavender soap from home.

This tub of water, which flows in and out, always fresh, is our gift from God.

I took a bath that very afternoon. I put on clean clothes and made my decision like a human being, not like a rat in captivity.

I would go to the hospital twice a week and write letters for the brave boys who needed them written. I felt good, making my decision.

But now there was another one to make. Something else was gnawing at my innards.

What to do about Robert.

For it was as clear to me as water in the cistern that I would have to do something. I could not leave it to Landon. He was too tied up with his honor codes, all twisted between his duty as a doctor and his duty as a soldier, to do anything.

Anybody who had honor like Landon had would always be in trouble.

So if something had to be done, I had to do it. Because he'd told me about it. He'd dragged me into it. And anyway, he was too busy. He had to report to Milliken's Bend hospital soon. And then what? Leave Robert here with us?

Suppose the authorities traced Robert down? And found him hidden away with the mother of a son who was with the Union army?

No. The more I thought about it, the faster my imagination worked. That's what comes from reading too much Edgar Allen Poe.

And whatever I did, I had to do it soon. I was unemcumbered by honor. My life wouldn't be ruined if I slipped Robert out of the scene.

It was still light when Landon left and about dusk when Mama called me aside. "Nobody knows but me and Easter and now you," she said.

Oh, good. More conspiracy. Just what I needed.

"The food is almost gone," she told me. "And I don't know what to do. I didn't want to tell Landon. He has enough on his mind. Mostly, it's you children I worry about. And Robert. He needs food if he's to get well. So I was thinking, Claire Louise, since the shelling has stopped for supper, can you take James and go on down by the creek and see if there are any blackberries left? I have enough meal for Easter to make some cornbread."

So James and I went off. It was a night in early June. And there is no finer thing made by God except maybe the look in a horse's eyes when she loves you. Apparently the balmy evening with the mild breeze moved everyone because once again we came across Confederates and Yankees visiting each other's campsites, exchanging coffee and cigars, and telling each other that if it were up to them, the enlisted men, they'd go home tomorrow.

I explained it all to James, who was very taken with the friendliness of the two sides now that the white flags were up once again. And disappointed. "Why don't they just pretend to be friendly and then kill each other?" he asked with all the wisdom of a five-year-old. "At least it'd save everybody a lot of time tomorrow."

I leaned down to hug him. Five-year-olds are so dear. Then James pointed a small finger at something behind me. "I think he's a Yank, Claire Louise," he said, "come to tell you something. Or give you something. He's got it in his hands."

I looked. Sure as God made apricots, it was a Yank. An officer no less, a lieutenant, if I knew my insignias right. And in his cupped hands he was holding something.

"Don't be scared, miss," he told me politely. "I just found this little fellow on the ground by that tree over there. And he looked in big trouble. Being a local girl, I thought you could take him home and nurse him until he gets strong enough to fly away."

He opened his hands just a bit, and inside I saw a bluebird looking up at me with the brightest and most kindly eyes. The lieutenant held his hands lower so James could see, too. "Hey," James said, "look at that. Can we take him home, Claire Louise? Can we?"

Afraid that he might start talking of home and who was in the cave with us and mention Robert, I quickly said yes. And there I went, laying the groundwork for trouble again.

"He's yours then," the lieutenant told James. "Here, where do you want to put him?"

I handed the bucket for the blackberries to James and picked up the ends of my apron, fashioning a bed for the bird. The lieutenant put him in and I closed the ends of the apron so he wouldn't fall out.

Then the lieutenant stood up straight and did something I never expected. He saluted us. "Thank you from the army of the United States," he said. Then he turned and walked away.

James was openmouthed. "Wow," he said. "Wait'll I tell Landon."

"Yes," I returned. Then I untied my apron in back, took it off, and fashioned a sort of bag out of it and handed it to James, cautioning him not to drop it. We picked our blackberries, then found our way home.

MAMA WAS happy about the blackberries and immediately asked Easter to make some corn muffins with blackberries in them. Everyone exclaimed over the bird and Easter found some cornmeal for it. I fashioned a nest out of an old cloth and it kept James busy all evening.

I saw several looks pass between Mama and Easter, but I did not know what for. Then, as she sometimes did, Mama asked me to take James downstairs and bathe him in the cistern, that he was the nearest thing to filthy she had ever seen. Robert, who could whittle, had made James a small boat for the cistern and so taking a bath was not such a chore anymore. The chore was getting him out. I let him stay about half an hour before I got him out, and by that time he was exhausted and near sleep when I put him in his pajamas.

I dried his hair good and carried him upstairs to his little room and put him to bed. No, he hadn't had any supper. At this point sleep was more important.

As I went down the hall and into the kitchen, Mama was just coming out, holding a tray with a bowl of soup on it. Next to the soup bowl was a dish of white meat. I stared.

She smiled. "For Robert," she said. "The soup will bring his strength back."

I don't know what made me realize what had happened. I just knew. Even before I looked around and saw Easter cleaning up the mess of blue feathers on the floor.

I gasped. "Mama! You didn't! *That was James's bird!*"

The smile never left her face. "Oh fiddlesticks, Claire Louise. Come now. You have to grow up sometimes. Anyway, what are we going to do with a bird in a cave?"

"Mama! Don't you care about anything anymore? That bird was James's new pet!"

"The cat would have eaten him," she retorted.

"I don't understand you, Mama. You've become so, so"—oh, I covered my face with my hands and started to cry—"uncaring!" I stamped my foot.

"Claire Louise! Apologize to Mama this minute! How dare you speak to her like that?"

Oh God, Landon, come in the front door. I'd heard someone come in, someone set something down, hard, on the floor, but in all my anguish, I hadn't paid mind. I sniffed and wiped my tears. I squared my shoulders.

"Do you know what she's done, Landon? Do you even care?"

"I care about one thing, Claire Louise, the way you're speaking to our mother. This war has done a lot of things to a lot of people. Good people. It has torn them apart, questioned their loyalties, turned their hearts, but when it starts turning members of a family against each other, it's time to lay down our arms and think what we're about. Now apologize." His voice was quiet, even, like Pa's.

He was getting more like Pa every day. Well, I decided, that wasn't such a bad thing to be like, was it? I did as he said. "I'm sorry, Mama," I said.

She compressed her lips, nodded her head. "So am I, daughter, sorry that I had to do this with the bird. Now just let me take this to Robert, and we can talk about it if you want." She walked past me, out of the kitchen.

James came running in then, past her. "What you got, Mama?" he asked.

"Some soup for Robert, so he can get better."

"Can I have some?"

Landon was across the kitchen in two strides. He picked up James and held him in his arms. "You wanna see what I've got here, Buddy? Look, I've brought food. All of this is food. For all of us. See? Look, bags of potatoes and corn and coffee, sugar and cans of sardines and pickles and big pieces of cheese and sides of bacon and—"

"Where'd you get it?" James asked.

"Well, my commanding officer said I could borrow a mule and take him and Rosie down to Chickasaw Bayou, to the river landing where supplies for our army are received. And I could take food for my family. Now and anytime in the future of this siege. So they won't starve. But we're not allowed to tell anybody. Got that?"

James nodded his head. "Mama cooked my bird and made soup out of it 'cause we had no food to make Robert strong," he said solemnly. "I heard everybody yelling about it."

Tears were coming down his face.

Landon wiped them away. "Yeah, but sometimes we have to make sacrifices in a war. Everybody does. Even down to a five-year-old boy," he told James.

"I'm a little man," James corrected him.

"Good. I'm glad to hear it. Then you mustn't cry. After the war, I'll make it up to you."

"How?" James wanted to know.

"Well, give me a chance and I'll see. Maybe I'll buy you a pony. How's that?"

James was ecstatic. He hugged Landon, who hugged him back, wholeheartedly. "Now come on, let's get this stuff out of the bag so Easter can make supper," he said.

CHAPTER ELEVEN

W HAT TO do about Robert.
Robert deserved a second chance, I decided.
Everyone did. So somehow he lost or dropped the order
from General Lee. Should a person die or be put into
prison for life for that? Should a person's life be ruined because of an innocent mistake?

Of course I could say no, because I was not in the
army. It did not have its tentacles wrapped around me. I
was not a doctor, with another whole barrel of fish to account for. And if I did what I wanted to do, no shame
would come down on my family.

But first, before I set out to become a heroine, I had
to get to know Robert, proper like. I had to at least spend
some time with him and find out what he was about.

We were at breakfast. We had food now, anyway,
thanks to Landon. No one was to know it, of course. It
was to be shared with no one. This was difficult. No one
was to know that Landon had been treated "special" and
allowed to bring his family food. For the simple reason,
he'd been told by his commanding officer, that the Yankee

army believed that the only way it would finally take Vicksburg was to starve its people out.

Mama said, "The idea of starving our neighbors out, while we eat in plentitude, bothers me, Landon."

"You want me to leave off bringing food, Ma?" he asked.

Landon could always come up with a reply that made you stand by your statements and abide by them, even while they squirmed beneath your feet.

"You know better," Mama said. "I've got to take care of my family."

Mama looked at him, long and hard. "The Yankees know that's the only way they'll get the city, don't they? Our soldiers can hold them off as long as they want to. We can't be beat with shelling. Only with starvation."

We ate in silence for a while then. Everyone but Robert. He wasn't eating.

"Did you decide whether you're going to work at writing those letters for our boys?" Mama asked me.

I nodded yes. "I've got to do something. I just can't sit around and do nothing," I told her.

"All right. I'll send a courier with a note to Dr. Balfour this morning that you'll come."

"I need you this morning, too," Landon announced. "I've got three patients due in the surgery. You can come over and play nurse and receptionist."

"I was going to read some Dickens to Robert this morning."

"Robert can wait." He winked at his friend. "He can have you when I'm finished. All right, old friend?"

Robert said it was all right. He was tired anyway, he said. Neither he nor Landon knew that this was the day I'd picked to get to know him.

I DIDN'T mind helping Landon in Pa's surgery. He didn't ask me to do much except take the patients' names and ailments down in the waiting room, then bring them into the surgery in order of their arrival.

"How's your pa?" they all asked me.

I told them we'd received only two letters, that he couldn't give out his destination but that he was with General Lee and in good health and said he would write to us soon. They all missed him.

"Landon's a good doctor," I told them.

They came with all kinds of ailments, from poison ivy to deep coughs, from sprained wrists to earaches. One woman came, she said, because she had nervous spasms from the sounds of the shelling, and she wanted to see if the young Dr. Corbet was as good as his father.

Once I had escorted the patient inside the surgery and fetched what Landon wanted, he would not let me stay. About six patients came that Saturday morning, even while we were being shelled and cannonaded and the musketry exploded overhead, and added to this treacherous music was the smashing of windows in nearby houses from the percussion of the explosions.

Landon dismissed me before noon to go and have lunch. But first I took him a tray fixed by Clothilda. He was as if lost in that surgery, time frozen for him.

WHEN I returned to the cave, Mama asked me to take a tray to Robert. I watched him eat. He liked rice and mushrooms, and Mama had made him his own concoction. But he didn't eat much.

"Your brother is convinced I have brain fever," he told me quietly, "but the only fever I have is to go home."

"I can understand that," I said.

"Suppose the quinine won't break the fever. You think your brother will let me go anyway?"

I had no way to answer. Landon told me, only last evening when we were putting away the food he'd brought, that he'd decided he had to turn Robert over to Pemberton. "It's the worst thing I've ever had to do," he'd said, "but it's the only thing I can do in my position."

"Your mother was in here this morning giving me a decoction of sprigs and leaves from the hemlock spruce tree," Robert was saying. "She asked your brother first, of course. He said yes. I think I'm feeling better. But how will we know whether it was the quinine or her remedy if the fever breaks?"

I smiled. "My mother often has that problem with Pa," I told him. "They always decide it doesn't matter as long as the patient gets well."

He then asked me to tell him about Pa, so I did. He

listened carefully, then told me about his pa, a plantation owner, now under the Yankees, since Jackson, Mississippi, was captured a while back. He told me about his own little sister, Cassie Lea, who could ride better than he could, and about his brother, Billy, who had been in a military academy before the war and now, at only seventeen, had joined up with the army and had a thirst for Yankee blood. He told me how he longed for some of his mammy's biscuits and ham and chocolate cake.

"My pa hates the Yankees with a passion," he told me. "Wait'll I tell him that my new friend is a Yankee and how he saved me."

I went solemn.

"What's wrong, Claire Louise? Did I offend you in any way?"

I shook my head. He really did think Landon was going to save him.

The realization came down on me like a mortar shell, exploding in shards and lights all around me. The noise made me unable to focus. Robert was mouthing some more of his truths.

"Did Andy give you any money?" I asked him outright.

He looked startled at first, then he understood. "Yes. He hired himself out and worked for it and gave it to me. How did you know?"

"I was there when he asked my brother if he could. He said it was for your trip home."

"Yes, I have enough, thank you."

"You'll need some food to take along. And someone to accompany you on the way out of town. To show you the best way, where you won't be hit by shells and bothered by people. Eight o'clock at night is the best time. Everyone is out then and one more person seen 'round and about won't be noticeable."

"You sound as if you discussed this with your brother. Did you?"

I picked up his lunch tray from the bed. The book *Great Expectations* lay there next to it. I admired the gold title on the cover. We hadn't even opened it.

"No, we haven't discussed it," I said. I took a deep breath. It might as well be now, I told myself. And so I told him.

"You won't like this, Robert. And you won't believe it. But it's true. Your friend, Landon, isn't going to help you escape. He's going to turn you in to Pemberton before he reports to Milliken's Bend hospital. I heard him tell Mama. He doesn't want to. But he can't do anything else in his position as a doctor and a captain in the Yankee army. You see, you're his prisoner, technically. He told me that if he helps you escape, he's an accessory to your running away and could be court-martialed."

He just stared at me. His eyes were so blue, and into the blueness now came tears, but he kept them in check, he wouldn't let them overflow.

"Claire Louise Corbet, are you funnin' me?" he asked.

"No, sir. No. I'm not. I wish I were. I've been thinking about it, you see, and I decided I want to help you escape. I want to help you get home. To your own mama and pa and Cassie Lea and those biscuits and ham and that chocolate cake. Even if the Yankees there make you a prisoner. Because it'll all end soon, and if you're a prisoner of Pemberton's it won't end, ever."

The silence stretched between us like we were pulling taffy. He was taking it all in. I could tell by his eyes, by the way he was slowly nodding his head.

And then he said something that summed it all up. "You love that brother of yours, but you're making your own decision, because you know it's the right thing to do," he said gravely. "I hope someday my sister, Cassie Lea, will have the sense you have."

"So you'll let me help you then?"

"Have at it, Claire Louise. What would you have me do?"

"You've only to be dressed and ready. I'll give you a sack of food and a Colt Navy revolver that was Pa's from the house. I'll walk you as far down as the spring where we met, where I was picking blackberries. I'll draw a map that will take you east from there."

"When?"

I paused only a moment. "In two nights," I said. "At the eight o'clock respite from shelling. Landon will likely be in Pa's surgery then. It's when people come. All right?"

"He'll punish you when he finds out."

"He won't find out. The lie is that you left on your own. You just picked up and skedaddled. I know how to lie, don't worry. I have to go now. Get plenty of rest and try to eat good between now and then."

He was perplexed, taken with the audacity of it. For one of Lee's officer's, I thought, he was powerful innocent. He must have come reluctantly to new plans.

I left.

CHAPTER TWELVE

I HAD A little scare late that afternoon when Landon called me aside and asked me why I had spent so much time with Robert after lunch.

The look of surprise on my face was real. How did he know? Had Mama told him?

"I hope you're not getting overfriendly with him," he cautioned.

"What is that supposed to mean?"

"I think you know."

"Well, damn."

"Don't use foul language with me."

And there he was, in an instant, up on his high horse. And there is nothing you can do about it when Landon gets up on his high horse, except wait until he is ready to get down.

"You were the one who said we were supposed to make him feel at home."

"His spirits are low, Claire Louise. And with good reason. He misses home. He doesn't know what's coming next. He's like a man drowning. He'll accept any rope thrown to him. Right now I'm that rope. Don't take it away from him."

Whatever that meant, it was an order as if it had come straight down from General Grant. And the look in Landon's eyes was the seal on the order. I nodded and we parted.

MAYBE, I thought, *maybe I should do it tonight.* I allowed the idea to tantalize me until I could stand it no more. And then, with no other purpose in mind, with the eight p.m. reprieve in the shelling, and with Mama's permission, I walked over to our house.

To my surprise the place was quiet in the evening of a late June day. With no shelling I could hear the birds, the cicadas, and, in the distance, the tolling of a church bell. It all sounded so nice. The chickens in the yard clucked to me. I was surprised. Did we still have chickens? Then I heard movement and voices from the barn.

"She just come flyin' in, Massa Landon," Andy was saying, "stirrups aflappin', reins jumpin', just as pretty as you please, and then just as she gets here, I come out the back door an' she sees me and neighs and comes over and she says hello."

"What time was that?" my brother asked.

"Couple hours ago, suh. I give her food and water and she happy as a pig in mud. Doan seem to mind the shellin', suh. I guess she used to it."

I stood in the barn door adjusting my eyes to the dimness inside.

Sure enough there was Jewel. My horse, come home!

"Jewel!" I near screamed it, startling both Landon and Andy. Both turned and stepped aside as I ran forward to the front of the stall and reached up and hugged her. She knew me, of course. She whinnied and nuzzled me and I hugged her around the neck for a long time. "Oh, Jewel, you're home."

"Did no one come looking for her?" Landon was asking.

"No, suh. Nobody. I think she jus' skedaddled from wherever she wuz and come back to her own barn. And them Yankees, excuse me, suh, but them Yankees too dumb to know where that is."

Landon tried to control a smile. And then I saw she was wearing a Yankee saddle and blanket. And so I went around and into the stall and unfastened the saddle, without saying a word. And I took off the blanket. Landon and Andy watched me. Everything was all right until I fetched one of our own blankets and saddles and put them on her.

"What do you think you're about?" Landon asked.

I didn't answer.

"Take that off. She isn't to be ridden for a while. Give her a rest."

I ignored him. I intended, you see, to have her ready for whenever I took Robert down to the stream. It wasn't a long way, but I might have to take him well beyond.

"Claire Louise, do as I say."

More ignoring on my part. After all she was my horse,

given to me by Pa, wasn't she? I just flung him a superior look. "I may ride her tomorrow morning," I told him.

What could he do? When it came down to it, nothing. I'd never pushed him to the edge to find out how far he would go. And I wasn't about to test his mettle, not here and now in front of Andy, anyway. He was too much of a gentleman to do anything in front of Andy. No one in my family ever displayed any unpleasantness in front of the servants.

"We'll talk about this later," he said.

All I knew was that I didn't want any Yankee blanket or saddle on Jewel.

Landon went around to Jeffrey's stall. Jeffrey was Robert's horse, and Landon checked on a bandage on his right front foot. I hadn't seen it before. "Try to keep him quiet today," he instructed Andy. He stood up, patted the horse's flanks, and was gone without so much as a fare-thee-well to me.

I felt a pang of panic. "What's wrong with Jeffrey?" I asked Andy.

He shrugged. "That horse come up limpin' t'other day after prancin' 'round in the pasture," he told me. "Your brother wuz here couple of times, fixin' him. I been awaitin' to tell you, Miz Claire Louise. That horse never gonna make it all the way to Jackson for that Confederate officer feller."

I felt my face go white. Of course Andy was in on this. Hadn't he earned the money to give to Robert for his escape? "How much have you told my brother about his plans to leave?" I asked him.

"Ain't said nuthin' 'cept 'bout earnin' the money, Miz Louise. Kept my mouth shut since you told me you wuz plannin' on makin' off wif him soon."

"Do you know why?"

"No, but I 'spose you got your reasons. An' I think it's right he shud go. 'Specially since I heard your brother say he was thinkin' of turnin' him over to the 'thorities. Doan know what he done, but he seem like a powerful nice boy, and I think he shud have another chance. So I'm wif you. When you goin'?"

"I had planned night after tomorrow."

"Tha's good. Make it fast. Too much dillydallyin' gets a body nowheres quick. You need me, you know you gots me."

"I need you to have both Jeffrey and Jewel ready here."

His eyes widened. "You ain't gonna go runnin' off wif him, is you, Miss Claire? That would kill your mama. An' your brother, he have half the Yankee army after you all."

"No, Andy. I'm only taking him as far as the creek."

"I be ready, Miz Claire Louise. I be ready."

CHAPTER THIRTEEN

I SCARCE slept at all that night for my plotting. When I did sleep, my dreams were fractured things, coming and going in broken flashes, elusive, cutting themselves off at the knees and disappearing just when I thought I had a purchase on what they were all about.

Mama was sleeping, I knew that. So was Easter, in a small room next to her. Robert was reading. James was sleeping, and Landon was out on a mission of mercy, delivering Mrs. Rappaport's baby. I thought about how, when Pa was home and came in late from a house call, I would wait up for him with a pot of hot chocolate. I wondered what he was doing at the moment.

From outside came the usual sounds of mortars, musketry, and shells, then, in between somehow, the sound of people screaming a dreaded word.

"Fire! Fire!"

Of a sudden it seemed like the whole world around me woke, like a sleeping tiger who'd been disturbed. Mama came looking for me and we met in the hallway. "What is it? Where is the fire?"

She had in her arms her daytime clothes.

Chip, who usually slept outside the entrance, had taken this night off. Now he came to alert us. "Ma'am, Washington Street is in flames. People all runnin' down dere to help. Captain Beggs of the fire brigade already be dere."

"Washington Street. Oh! Claire Louise, isn't that where Landon went?"

"Yes, ma'am."

"I must get dressed. Chip, you accompany me. Easter, you stay with the children and Robert. Keep them safe."

"Yes, ma'am," Easter said.

"The whole street," Chip was saying, "from Brown and Johnston to Crutcher's store be burnin'. Captain Beggs tryin' to get as many people as he can to put it out."

"Well, when we get there you can help, after you help me find Landon," Mama said.

I slipped into Robert's room while she was dressing in hers. "Robert," I whispered, "I'm thinking that now, *this very hour*, would be the time to spirit you out of here. With all the confusion nobody would know the difference."

He nodded. "I was thinking the same thing. But how do we make our exit?"

"Claire Louise?" Mama called. "Where are you?"

I stepped out into the hall. "I was talking to Robert, Mama. He thinks that during all this confusion is when people do a lot of looting. He says that Andy and Clothilda will likely go to the fire and answer Captain Beggs's call. Robert says he is well enough to go to our house and hold off any intruders."

Mama was lacing up her blouse in front. She came to the doorway of Robert's room. "Are you sure you're up to it, Robert? My son would never forgive me if you fainted on the way there."

"Claire Louise can accompany me, ma'am," he said. "But yes, I'm up to it. I've got my sidearm. And the house will be looted if someone isn't there to protect it."

God bless him. God bless you, Robert.

"Well, don't just stand there," Mama snapped at me, "get yourself dressed, young lady. Since when do you prance about in your nightclothes in front of a man if he isn't your brother?"

"Mama, why is everybody yelling so? They woke me up."

James now. Mama knelt down and told him about the fire and how Easter was going to stay with him here until she came right back with Landon and, if he was good, Easter might even tell him stories. Would he like that?

"I want to hear about Br'er Rabbit and Br'er Fox," he said.

"Claire Louise, go in the kitchen and make me up a basket of food to bring for Landon. He hasn't had any supper."

I got worried then. Things were falling into place too easily for me. I went into the kitchen and made up a basket of food for Landon and one for Robert, too, which I wrapped in a small tablecloth.

CHAPTER FOURTEEN

W<small>E DREW</small> the night around us as we began the walk to our house. In the west where the town was on fire, the sky was streaked with a fearful red. We were downwind from it and so we breathed in smoke and ashes floated in front of our eyes.

Robert said something to me but I don't know what. People were rushing past us, everyone going the other way. No one paid us mind. My brain was working furiously. *But Andy said his horse could never make the trip. His front leg is all bandaged. Landon attended to it. What will you do?*

"Your house looks deserted," Robert said.

There it loomed, ahead of us. Its familiar form like a comforting shape ready to enfold us. But there was no one about, so we went straight to the barn. And then Robert embraced Jeffrey. The horse whinnied his hello and Robert saw the foreleg.

"What happened?" he asked.

"My brother says he'll be all right with time. Andy says he was prancing about in the field back there and stepped into a hole. But Andy also says he won't be all right for the trip."

"Then what are we doing here?" he asked.

Yes, what? But I knew. In places inside me where I hadn't gone yet, I knew.

"You'll take Jewel," I told him. And even as I said the words I felt as if I were cutting little pieces out of myself and giving them away. But there was no stopping now that I'd set my course. You can't take back words like that. The angels have already got them and have taken them away.

Then I saw the look on Robert's face and I didn't want to.

After all, we weren't playing a game here. He had to get away. Run away. There was the whole thing in a nutshell. If he didn't do it tonight, most likely he'd never have the chance again. We'd been given this chance, and if we were too dense to take it, well it was nobody's fault but our own.

I felt that if we didn't take it now, my brother might turn Robert in tomorrow. Or the day after. He soon had to report to Milliken's Bend. He didn't have too many tomorrows left, either.

None of us did.

Landon would be angry at me, of course, when he found out I'd helped Robert skedaddle. It would be, in Landon's eyes, a capital offense. The trick was not to let him know I'd helped. Lie. He'd go back to the army never knowing, perhaps to be transferred again. The army seemed obsessed with this transferring stuff.

"Do you want Jewel to take this saddle?" Robert was asking.

"Yes, and the blanket. Everything."

He smiled. "I'll lead her on foot so's you can walk next to me. People will think we're going to see the fire."

"No they won't, because we're not going in that direction. We're going by way of the stream. From there, it's a straight path to the other back paths that will take you to Jackson. Nobody but wounded and sick like you will you meet. Soldiers who have had enough and are going home."

"I'll know the way. I've ridden up there to Vicksburg before."

I gave him a half smile, but there were tears in my eyes. He smiled back as he checked the cinch of the saddle. Then he secured the bundle of food and gave Jewel a carrot.

We both noticed, at the same time then, that the shelling had stopped. The churches' bells in Vicksburg were tolling. Robert cleared his throat. "The Yankees have the decency, at least, not to shell our people when they're trying to put a fire out."

"Yes."

We looked at each other for a moment. And then we left.

We were nowhere near Washington Street, yet people continued to rush past us, carrying blankets and driving wagons and even food for those who'd been hurt in the fire. I wondered where Mama had ended up, what Landon was doing. Had Mrs. Rappaport had her baby?

Would Landon be back to our house in a little while to open the surgery to treat people hurt in the fire? We must be gone from here then. I told Robert and we hurried away from the vicinity of home.

We walked down toward the stream where I'd picked blackberries. I thought of the many mornings I'd come here with Pa, the gentler times. I thought of what he'd say about all of this. It was a clear night, with stars in their appropriate places, and we walked unhurriedly now to our destination. Nobody looked at us as we passed them on the street. There were no words of friendliness. I saw two of Pa's women patients, laden with a basket of food, the father of one carrying blankets, but none even nodded at me.

We were suddenly in a world full of strangers.

"It's too bad you couldn't have taken the railroad," I said to Robert.

He grunted. "Too many officers of both armies traveling. You need identification. They'd have me in a minute."

Robert was right. He was better off staying to himself, out of sight.

"You'll take care of Jewel for me, won't you?" I tried to keep the tears out of my voice.

"Word of honor," he said. Then he gave a short, bitter laugh. "If it matters any coming from a person the whole Confederate army is looking for."

"I still think you'd be better off in civilian clothes. I could have gotten you some of Landon's back at the house."

"Thanks again, Claire Louise, but if I hang, I'd rather it not be as a spy."

We came to the ravine where the stream was. Jewel

whinnied, smelling water. Carefully we made our way down and let her drink.

I pointed out the path on the other side of the ravine that he should take, bypassing the town and all the activity around it. I gave him the directions that I'd written down. They would keep him away from the public road, on the edge of the woods, yet parallel with the Vicksburg and Jackson railroad tracks.

He looked down at me. "You're going to be quite a woman, Claire Louise," he said. "'S'matter of fact, you already are. You've grown up heaps since I've been here. Just this here act of giving me your horse is a sure sign of it. There're lots of grown-ups who wouldn't do a thing like this."

I felt myself blushing.

"After the war, whether I live through all this or not, I'd like you to make a visit to Charltonsville and come see us. That's the name of our plantation."

It also, I thought to myself, *is your papa's name, isn't it? Charlton.*

"I'm going to tell my folks all about you. They'll know who you are. And they'll take good care of Jewel."

"You think you'll be caught, Robert?"

"I may have to move away," he said.

It was all getting to be too much for me. I threw my arms around Jewel's neck and said good-bye to her. She knew. Darned horse, she knew we were parting. "You're going on a mission for me," I whispered to her. "You do good now, you all hear?" I patted her velvet nose. I kissed her. She whinnied again.

Now I didn't care about the tears in my eyes, or if Robert saw them.

He held me by the shoulders for a minute, steadying me, and then he leaned down and kissed me.

It was not a brotherly kiss as Landon would give. How can I describe what it was? It was gentle, yet intrusive. Chaste yet knowing. When he finished, he looked down at me. "You better get back," he said.

I knew I should protest. I knew if my brother were here that kiss would be sufficient for Landon to call him out. I knew I should probably slap him for being bold.

But I did nothing. I said nothing. This was good-bye.

"Claire Louise, I could love you," he said. Then he turned away. "I'll take care of Jewel," he said. "Don't worry your pretty little head about that."

And while I stood there like a jackass in the rain, he walked Jewel up the other side of the ravine and was about to disappear into the woods when he stopped again. "Thank you for this," he said. "I'll try, somehow, to get her back to you."

The last I saw of them was Jewel's white tail swishing on her golden body.

CHAPTER FIFTEEN

S o THERE I was, alone in the ravine, like I was at the bottom of the world, with all the quiet in the world above me. *Quiet is nice,* I thought. I looked up for the stars, but there was only smoke, and that made me pull myself out of my reverie and decide what to do next.

I could go back to the cave. Or I could go back to the house.

I decided on the house, because I'd promised Mama that Robert and I would guard it against looters. I went up the side of the ravine and got my bearings and started home, wondering what I would do if the house was already looted. I walked home, making up lies along the way. Without Jewel I felt like I was missing my right arm. I wondered what she thought, taking Robert home. Horses think, I knew that. There were plenty of instances when I had proof that Jewel was thinking.

The house, when I got to it, was dark, no candles in the windows, no lanterns anywhere. It was downright creepy going in that front door, into the center hall. Of course I knew everything so well I could have walked through the place blindfolded, but that wasn't the point. The point was nobody was home! And this was my home! And right now it was full of ghosts, and I wanted my family to be here like they'd been before that fool Grant and his army attacked us.

I pulled myself together. "You can allow yourself only two minutes of self-pity," Pa had said. "Then you must get on with it."

Pa. He was ailing. Ma had had a letter from him just this past week, telling her he was on his way home. No, he hadn't lost any arms or legs. He was all of a piece, but he had what they were calling camp fever, and they were sending him on home to recuperate.

Pa with camp fever! He'd never been sick a day in his life. Oh, my whole world was falling apart.

I found my way down the hall and out back to the kitchen, where I groped around for a lantern. Beside it Clothilda always kept some of Landon's matches. I managed to strike one and light the lantern. It sent a warm glow through the place. Now all I needed was one of Pa's Colt Navy revolvers.

Into Pa's study and to his gun case. There he kept his guns, not many, an old hunting rifle, a few Colt Navy handguns. As I thought it would be, the glass-enclosed case was locked.

Where was the key? Likely Mama had it hidden away somewhere. If I wanted a handgun, I'd have to break the glass. Well, if Robert and I were guarding the house, as I'd promised we were going to do, we'd have to break the glass, wouldn't we?

I turned to Pa's desk, found a paperweight, and hit the glass with it. The sound of splintering glass is never pleasant, but in the dark, empty house it sounded sickening. I reached my left hand in for the Colt Navy, secured it, and on pulling it out, cut my hand, right above the thumb.

"Peabrain," I called myself. I set the revolver down on Pa's desk and grabbed the hem of my dress to douse the blood, but it wouldn't be doused.

I picked up the revolver again, went back into the kitchen, took up a small towel, and wrapped my hand in it. There. I'd learned something helping Landon in Pa's surgery, hadn't I?

Then I went into the front parlor, just off the main hall, and sat in a chair, the revolver in my lap, holding my throbbing hand and watching the shadows on the walls from the pine-knot torches people carried as they passed the house. And I promptly fell into a disturbed sleep.

In back of my mind I heard Mama's grandfather clock at the foot of the stairway in the hall chime out the hour. Twelve midnight. I was jerked awake. Where was I? Then I remembered and fell asleep again.

The next time I was jerked awake some people were standing over me. "Claire Louise, where's Robert?" from Landon.

"And what did you do to your hand?" from Mama.

It took me only a moment to adjust my mind to what was going on around me. I looked down at my hand. Blood had soaked through the towel and part of my skirt was red.

"Come along with me," Landon was saying.

"I'll get a clean skirt and petticoat," I heard Mama say.

"Where are we going?" I asked shakily.

"To Pa's surgery. To stitch up that hand."

"How do you know it needs to be stitched up?"

"Do you prefer to bleed to death?" He sounded annoyed.

In back of the house we went through the door to Pa's surgery.

But first we had to go through the waiting room.

It was then that I saw the bird.

There were about six or eight people waiting in all variations of distress, from broken bones to cut faces.

Also three Yankee soldiers holding rifles were standing around another Yankee soldier who was holding a perch attached to a wooden pole.

On the perch was a bald eagle. I stopped and stared at them. So did Landon for a minute. "Is this Old Abe?" he asked them.

"Yeah, Doc. He got skinned in the leg. We need him fixed. People told us to go and find the Yankee doctor. Be that you?"

"Yes," Landon answered evenly.

"Will you fix him up for us, Doc?"

"If you will set down your guns and let me attend to

this bleeding girl first," Landon answered. "I won't be long. Give your names and regiment to my mother here."

"Company C/8th Regiment, Wisconsin Volunteers," one of them recited. Mama took it down and handed me my clothing, a clean skirt and petticoat and pantalets.

Landon took my arm and led me into the surgery.

"Doctor, Doctor, Doctor," they appealed, as we passed through.

"Be with you in a minute," Landon said. "My sister here has cut her hand, badly."

Landon closed the door and gestured that I should sit.

"How'd you get the cut?"

"Breaking into Pa's gun case for a revolver."

He unwrapped the towel and gestured I should come to the sink, where he poured something over the cut that stung so bad it made me cry. "I'm sorry," he said. Why was it that I didn't believe him?

"You telling me that you've been bleeding like this for the whole night?"

"No. Just for a couple of hours."

"You've been here only a couple of hours then. I'm going to sprinkle some laudanum on this so it doesn't hurt when I stitch it up. That's an ugly cut you've got there."

He sprinkled it on. Then he got his needle and started to stitch. I wanted to cry out in pain, but I wouldn't let myself. I couldn't control my legs though. They were giving way under me. Not so much from pain as from the sight of him stitching.

I suppose I would have slumped to the floor just as he finished his stitching if he hadn't picked me up like I was a rag doll and put me on the table. I was sitting there and he stood directly in front of me. "What did you do before you cut the hand?" he said.

He was wrapping it now, gently.

"I don't remember."

"You don't lie very well."

"Is this the way you treat your patients?"

There was silence between us. He gave it time to move across the heavens, like clouds across the sky. He was still wrapping the hand. "What happened to Robert?" he asked again, concentrating on the bandage and not looking at me.

"I don't know."

"I've got no time for lies. I was going to turn Robert over to the authorities, yes. It was the right thing for me to do. No one in the Confederacy will ever know now who lost that order of Lee's and a few people will always be under suspicion. A few lives ruined. Do you think that's right?"

I didn't answer.

He sighed. It was deep and sad. "When I put Rosie in the barn, I saw that Jewel was gone. You did a big thing tonight, giving Robert your horse. I know you think you did the right thing, but it was wrong. It was none of your affair, and it was wrong."

Tears were coming down my face.

"Do you really think he's going to go home? Where he can be found? He'll likely go West, where all the fugitives from this war will go. Claire Louise, I'm going to ask you one more time. Not with the intention of having him run down. But for us. To save what we have. Had. What happened to Robert?"

I felt like a fox in a leg trap. Did he have to make his voice so kind? So gentle? I shook my head. Tears were really coming down my face now.

"You haven't anything to say to me then. All right." He handed me my clean clothes. "Change in here. I don't want you going through the waiting room and all those patients seeing you covered with blood."

He helped me down from the table and went to one corner of the surgery and drew a curtain across it. "Here. For your modesty. If you think you're going to faint, call me. Remember, I'm a doctor."

I went into the corner. He had a grip on the curtain. He was about to close it when he stopped. "Oh," he said, "one more thing. If you don't tell me what I want to know tonight, then I don't want you ever to tell me. Someday when we're both old and sitting around drinking a mint julep and our grandchildren are picking blackberries down by the stream, you can tell me. And I can't see any reason why we have to be friends between now and then, either."

He closed the curtain with a dramatic movement and went to call in the three Yankee soldiers with the bald eagle.

I felt like I'd been slapped. I was stung so by the words. I commenced to cry again and I struggled to change. I felt weak. The back of my neck was in a cold sweat, as was my scalp. And my stomach felt queasy. But I'd faint dead on the floor before I'd call Landon in to help me, doctor or no doctor.

I listened to the exchange of words between him and the Yankees. One soldier was bragging how, when the 8th Wisconsin went into battle, Old Abe would fly over the fighting and screech at the enemy. "So many times those Rebs tried to shoot him and they'd miss," he told Landon. "Is he bad, Doc? Will you be able to fix his leg?"

"Sure will," Landon assured them.

I rolled my bloody clothes in a ball.

"You finished back there, Claire Louise?" Landon called out.

"Yes."

"Then you'd better skedaddle. I've got a heap of patients to see yet."

I stepped out from behind the curtain. "How's the hand?" he asked without looking at me. "Any more bleeding?"

"No, but it hurts precious bad."

He went to a cabinet and got some powders and put them in some paper and handed them to me. "Help you to sleep tonight," he said. "Take only one at a time. I suggest you go over to the hospital in a day or so and have Dr. Balfour take a look at it. I'll be gone tomorrow."

What was he telling me? I paused only a moment. "Can I pet the bird?" I asked.

The eagle blinked at me.

The soldiers nodded their head, yes, saying he liked women.

"No," Landon said. "This isn't a game we're playing. You'd best leave."

The soldiers looked embarrassed. He'd told them I was his sister, hadn't he? I'd heard it when I was behind the curtain. They knew he was a Southerner and were likely thinking, "I thought Southern families were close and loving."

I left, and as I did I heard him refusing to take money for fixing Old Abe. From the window in the center hall of the house I watched the Yankee soldiers, guns at the ready, walking down to the waterfront. Old Abe was secure on his perch.

CHAPTER SIXTEEN

I ASKED Mama if I could sleep in my own room in our house that night, and she said no, to go home to the cave, all we needed was there. But to wait until Landon was finished in his surgery so he could walk both of us back.

I said yes, then I walked back alone. Might as well be hanged for a lion as for a lamb, or however the saying went.

I wondered how Old Abe was faring, and if my brother had fixed him up so he could fly again. I felt a repeat of the anger I'd felt for Landon because he wouldn't let me pet the eagle. I knew it was his way of punishing me.

How many other ways, I wondered, *would he find, over the years.*

Years. Did he have it in him to let this go on for years? It wasn't so much the bald eagle, though it would have been one more thing to tell my grandchildren. It was the feelings that made him do it that saddened me so.

I went back to the cave and found it quiet and put

myself right to bed after taking the powder that Landon had given me.

THE NEXT morning low voices from the kitchen woke me. Landon and Mama. I didn't want to face either one of them now, so I dressed slowly, careful to put on my blue and white check and make one braid down the back with my hair because today I would be going to the hospital.

They were still at table when I went for my breakfast.

The Confederate dispatch rider had been in town early and Mama had a letter from Pa. She was glowing as she recited he'd be home in a day or two.

Landon, all spiffed up in his uniform, held James on his lap. Chip had Rosie waiting outside. "You going to be a good boy while I'm gone?" Landon asked James.

"No." James shook his head solemnly.

"Who's going to be man of the house when I'm away?"

"Pa's coming home in two days," James told him.

"Yes, but he's ailing. You have to take over until he's well."

"Do I get to tell Claire Louise what to do like you do?"

I put sugar in my coffee. I felt Landon's glance in my direction, but I did not return it.

"You can try," Landon says. "Maybe you'll have better luck than I've had." He put James from his lap and got up then and kissed Mama. "Take care, darling," he said to her. "If you need anything, if Pa gets bad, send for me."

He kissed the top of James's head, then looked at me. "Claire Louise, look at me."

I looked. What did he want now?

"I want you to behave. No shenanigans. Pa isn't well. Do your part. You hear?"

"Yes."

He nodded briefly, took up his things, but did not go out the door. There was going to be more. I waited.

"I don't want you inviting friends in. Or talking about any food or possessions we might have. Most other caves are barely an improvement on cow stalls. You hear me?"

I said yes. I heard. And he went out the door.

Something went with him. Something vibrant and right. I cannot name what it was. But there was a black hole in the cave, nevertheless, when he was gone.

IT WASN'T until after he left and Mama lingered over her tea and I over my bacon and scrambled eggs and bread that I saw the front page of the *Citizen,* printed on the back of a piece of wallpaper.

The date was Thursday, July 2. The story said that General Pemberton, in a council of war, had told his generals: "I am a northern man. I know my people. I know we can get better terms from them on the Fourth of July than on any other day of the year."

Pemberton was readying to surrender Vicksburg.

I looked at Mama. She nodded, sadly. "Landon says

we can't hold out any longer," she told me. "We're eating well, thanks to him, Claire Louise, but most of the people in town are starving. Molasses is ten dollars a gallon; flour, five dollars a pound; meal, a hundred and forty dollars a bushel, if you can get any of it."

"Why didn't Landon say anything at breakfast?"

"Why does anyone in this house say or not say anything, Claire Louise? You and Landon are both so moody, I can't keep up with you. Tell me, why aren't you two talking?"

I didn't answer.

"This is no time to fight. The war has torn everybody apart. You both had something wonderful together. Now it's gone. You must work to get it back, Claire Louise. Any of us could get killed, any day."

"Why do I have to work to get it back? What about him?"

"He has much on his mind. His work, his family. He kept us together all the while Pa was gone. He kept us alive with food, didn't he? He even treated people in Pa's surgery."

"And he treated a bald eagle, which he wouldn't let me pet, even though its owners said yes."

"I don't know anything about that, child."

"He did it to be mean, because I wouldn't tell him how Robert got away. And he said, if you want to know, that we will never be friends again." I started to cry. "And you want me to make it right with him? Why should I?"

"Because you're the woman," she persisted. "And that's part of a woman's job. When you wed someday, you will find out why. You'll have to do it to keep your marriage together. Men are stubborn creatures, the lot of them, Claire Louise. You have only to make the first step and see them come around."

"Is that what you did with Pa?"

"Many times, child."

I lowered my head. "I have to go to the hospital," I said, "before the shelling starts again."

There was a perfect excuse to get away. The shelling would start again in fifteen minutes.

I leaned over and kissed her. She held me close. "I know Landon really loves you, Claire Louise. He always did. He was only twelve when you were born, and he kept insisting that when the baby came he was going to be its father."

I picked up the page from the *Citizen*. "It says here that they need contributions of wallpaper if they're to continue publishing," I read to her. "Could I give them a piece of wallpaper from my bedroom at home, Mama? Could I please?"

"Now what do you want to do that for?"

"Because I want to do something that I can tell my grandchildren about someday. I haven't done anything important in the war so far. And now Pemberton is going to surrender the town. Oh please, Mama," I felt myself warming to the idea even as I spoke. "I'll just cut a small piece from my wall. We can put new paper up when the war is over."

"Now I call that destructive," she said.

"No, Mama, it's sacrifice. Something I did that nobody else in the family did. You've done things. So has Pa and Landon. Please, Ma? I'll be good if you let me. I'll be so good."

She eyes me narrowly. "Will you think about making things up with Landon?"

I hesitated only a second. Long enough to realize there was no way I could make things up with Landon. It was impossible. He'd never agree to it.

"Yes," I said.

So she said yes, only don't, she said, go ripping all the paper off the walls in your room. "That paper came from England, in better times. Lord knows when we'll be able to get some again."

THE HOSPITAL tent seemed twice as crowded as it had been two days ago. Dr. Balfour scarce had time to say hello to me.

"I don't even know half of the new ones yet," he said. "Later, I'll look at that hand of yours. Landon sent by a note. Said you should just talk to them if you can't write. Can you write?"

I was taken aback that Landon should give the time to write such a note about me. For a brief moment I had a glimmer of hope. Did he still consider me part of his family? How far did the boundaries of his disinterest go?

"Yessir, I can write," I told Dr. Balfour.

"Don't overdo it," he cautioned.

I wrote three letters that morning. One for an Irish boy who had a wife in Georgia and who'd had an arm amputated and was here for a fever that followed. "They think I'm gonna die," he said bitterly. "Well I don't aim to die. An' if they send a priest, tell the good Father I don't need him."

"Why can't you tell him?" I asked.

"'Cause, as soon's I write this letter to my wife, I aim to have a dose of this here whiskey a friend smuggled to me yesterday"—he reached his good arm under the cot and picked it up and showed it to me—"an' go into blue heaven land. An' I'll be there when the good Father comes in. An' I don't want to be waked. Sure'n it's what I deserve, considerin' what I gave for my country, isn't it?"

I agreed and set about taking down the letter.

The second one, I was just about to approach when a male nurse came up behind me. He was a colored man. "'Scuse me, Miss Corbet, but Dr. Balfour, he say, doan get any closer to this here man. He done got typhoid."

I looked into the nurse's kindly face, then past him to the far corner of the room where Dr. Balfour was looking toward us. He was waving me aside.

Then, from my place on the floor, about six feet from the bed, I looked at the young soldier with typhoid. "Oh, please, Miss, take down my words. They aren't much, but I've got to let my wife know I'm still alive."

I looked at the colored man. "Go and ask Dr. Balfour if I can do it standing here," I said. Then I waited while the male nurse made his way between the cots and conferred with the doctor. Then maneuvered his way back again.

"Doctor say you gonna be one difficult woman, and then Doctor say, okay, but not one step closer or he send for your brother right now."

That, according to Dr. Balfour, was the worst threat he could level at me. I nodded my head, yes. And since young Edward Baldwin overheard the whole thing and I didn't have to explain, he commenced dictating his love letter to his wife loud enough so that at least twelve other patients could hear it.

All talk around us stopped. No one moved. They all lay still and some had tears coming down their faces. And Edward Baldwin poured his heart out for all of them it seemed, especially when he said: "If I don't make it out of here, my dear Rosemary, I want you to know I will always be with you, no matter where you go or what you do. I will always be at your side. And we will meet again in heaven."

The third letter was for a man from "Nor' Kaaaliana, Miss. But afore you put my words to paper, kin you just somehow git me a biled sweet purtatur? I do so long for one. I ain't had a one since I left home an' my mama's cookin'."

I told him as soon as we got the letter written I'd ask the cook, but that I had a hurt hand and it was starting to throb and his was the last letter I could do today.

"Lord a'mercy, then cud you all jus' move me away from this here dead man in the cot next to me? I mean I wuz used to seein' men die on the field, but I thought this here hospital wasn't fer dyin' in. Please, Miss?"

I said yes and grabbed a nearby orderly who had heard the request and in five minutes the dead man was removed. Then we went about with his letter. And true to my word, I ventured into the kitchen, which was really just an adjoining tent, to order a "biled sweet purtatur" for my charge.

On the way back, at the far end of the tent near the kitchen, I saw her.

Sarah Clarke.

It *was* her, wasn't it?

What was she doing here? And then it came to me. It was Sarah Clarke, and she was sick or hurt. *Stupid*, I told myself. And she was *here*, right under our noses, and none of us knew it, maybe not even Dr. Balfour. He'd told me he didn't know all of them yet, hadn't he?

I stood, stunned for a minute, like I was nailed to the floor. And then I did what I knew I should do. I walked over to her bed. "Hello, Sarah."

I heard her gasp. I saw her adjust the bedclothes closer, as she must be accustomed to doing so people couldn't see her bosoms and know she was not a man.

Or was it so that people couldn't see that one arm was amputated up to the elbow?

"Hello, Claire Louise," she said.

Our eyes met. She held my look. I wet my lips, which had gone dry. She gave a little grin and gestured with her head to my bandaged hand.

"You join up, too?"

"No, I cut it trying to get a revolver out of Pa's gun case. It's a long story. What about you?"

"I got hit with shell fragments. Skirmish near Mc-Connellsburg, Pennsylvania. Isn't that a kick in the head? I wanted to make it to Gettysburg. They're still fighting over there, I hear." She sighed. "Well, they fixed me up in the tent hospital, then shipped me here on the train. I didn't want to come. But I had no say in the matter. They found out I was a woman and I was cashiered out. Look here, Claire Louise, you can't tell anyone I'm back. Nobody. My family's not around, so I don't worry about them. But don't tell yours. And especially not Landon. I'd rather they cut off my other arm before he knew."

I drew in my breath and let it out slowly. "More secrets," I said.

"What?"

"Landon and I are, well, to be polite call it estranged. We scarce talk. And all because of secrets. I can't do that anymore, Sarah. No, I'm not going to go home, to your house or mine, and tell everybody you're here. But if it comes to dueling at twenty paces to protect your secret, I won't play that game, that's what I'm saying."

"What happened between you and Landon? Was it on account of me?"

"No."

"Where is he?"

"Doctoring at Milliken's Bend hospital."

"Thank God. They almost sent me there. Look, I understand your plight. I don't want to drag you into my affairs. Just give me a couple of days. I have a slight fever, which can follow an amputation. It was only done four days ago. I'm going to ask the nurse for some medicine and make sure I eat good and skedaddle out of here first chance I get."

"You mean you're running away?"

"That's what I mean. I don't ever want Landon to see me like this. I'm going to the depot and catching the train. I'll be gone in two days."

"Can I get anything for you?"

"No. Just stay out of it, sweetie. When all of this is over, maybe we'll see each other again. Don't worry about me. The war has toughened me up. Go now, before you get in trouble. Oh, and the story I'm giving old Balfour there is that I don't want my family to know, either, yet. I'm going to an aunt's house in Raymond. All right?"

Raymond. It was below Jackson. "Yes," I said. But it was not okay. There was something wrong here. Something all wrong. And I had to think about it in the open air, and not be muddleheaded this time.

CHAPTER SEVENTEEN

I LEFT the hospital at noon, just as the shelling stopped, and walked to our house, determined to get that piece of wallpaper, determined to put my mind to what I was going to do now about Sarah, determined to test my mettle and *not* tell anyone I happened to meet about her being home.

I let myself in the house and went straight to the kitchen to get a pair of scissors and a knife.

Neither Clothilda nor Andy was home. It was strange to have the house so silent. It was filled with spirits. I felt it right off. The grandfather clock stood guard in the hall, chiming away the hours as if there were somebody who cared. I went upstairs to my bedroom.

The glass on a back window was shattered because of heavy shelling, but otherwise there was no real damage. Some items had fallen off my dressing table. I looked around and decided to take the paper from the wall by the shattered window.

It was not a difficult job, except for my injured hand. I had to move slowly and carefully, but soon I had a whole sheet of wallpaper, from ceiling to floor. I rolled it up, pleased with myself, then went downstairs, put away the knife and the scissors, and went on my way to the newspaper office.

It was on Crawford Street, two blocks west of Dr. Balfour's home. As I approached I could see that the building itself had been hit several times with shells. The large front window was boarded up. I tried the front door. It was open. I went in.

"Be careful of the floor," called a voice from the back. "Don't fall through."

I looked down and sure enough in several places the floor wasn't there and the boards around it were blackened as if burned.

Mr. Swords came forward, grave, middle-aged, and wearing a cap with a visor. "We been hit several times. My type has twice been scattered all over the floor. You're the little Corbet girl, aren't you? Your pa's away. How's the rest of your family?"

When I saw the condition of his newspaper office, I had to say "fine, thank you." After all, here was a man who was fighting his own war against the Yankees, a man they couldn't burn out, smash out, or drive out. He went right on publishing his words. Don't have any more newsprint? Well, I'll just ask the folks for wallpaper.

"I brought you some wallpaper, Mr. Swords."

He exclaimed over it. He said it would comprise the first page of tomorrow's edition. "July third, tomorrow," he said, lowering his voice. "My scouts tell me that the white flags are going up. There's going to be a truce while Grant and Pemberton talk.

"It isn't surrender, Claire Louise. It's just common sense. We're out of everything. Our soldiers are weak and starving. So are our citizens. We have nothing left to hope for or fight with. What we do is an honorable thing." He took the wallpaper from me and smiled. "I'll save a copy for you," he said. "I've already got people asking me for copies to save for future generations. You come by when it's all over. Yours will be in this bottom drawer of my desk." He pulled out the drawer so I could see. "Your name will be on it."

"Thank you, Mr. Swords."

"Thank you, child. You'd best get home now. Give my best to your family."

I WENT right home, and when I got to the door of our cave, I was surprised and frightened to see Mercer, Pa's horse, tethered outside.

Pa was home!

All thoughts of surrender of Vicksburg and my wall-paper, my injured hand, and the possibility of resumed shelling, fled. Pa was home. All would be right with the world.

I went inside.

He was there, seated at the dining table, having a cup of real coffee with real sugar in it. Ma was there, too.

James was on his lap. He had his coat off and it was thrown aside with his sword and sidearm and hat.

He looked up as I came in. "Ah, here she is. Our wandering letter writer," he said. His voice was just a little weak. His face just a little pale.

I stared at him for a minute, imprinting him on my mind. "Hello, Pa," I said.

It had been a long time since that night in the church basement when he'd said good-bye to me. A lot had happened. I felt as if I'd traveled a great distance through a tunnel and was only now starting to see the light at the other end.

He set James off his lap and I went to him. "No kisses," he said. "I don't know yet what kind of foul fever I've got."

"I see you still do as you're told," he murmured in my ear when I didn't kiss him. "How are you, Claire Louise?"

"I'm fine, Pa."

"Where have you been? Your mother's been worried about you. She says you often wander about town without telling her where you're going."

I stood straight in front of him. "I was at the hospital, writing letters. Then I went home to cut a piece of wallpaper to give to Mr. Swords because he needs some to print his paper on, and Mama said I could do it. And then I took it to his office, which has been hit so many times by shells. Oh, it's just terrible, Pa! And then I came home."

He was eyeing me, the way he did when he listened to

you and read between the lines. He could tell if you were lying if you swore on a stack of bibles in front of you.

I purposely did not mention Sarah Clarke. It wasn't lying if I just didn't talk about her, was it?

I didn't mention her because it was such a big thing that she was back and she was lying in that hospital bed with one arm destroyed and talking about taking the train and running away that my mind had not yet accepted it.

What to do? Get word to her family and my brother and make a riot?

Say nothing and let her go so she's never found again? Like I did with Robert?

Or seek out Landon and tell him? Use her for my own ends, to make things up with Landon?

Suppose Landon didn't care anymore. Suppose he said, "Let her go, I don't care."

Suppose he was repelled by her cut-off arm.

Landon wouldn't be like that, I told myself. He's a doctor. It won't bother him. He loves her.

But what will he think of me? Using Sarah to get back in his good graces. He'll think I'm a humbug, I told myself. Won't he?

Well, he thinks I'm worse now. So I might as well be hanged for a sheep as for a lamb, or however the saying goes.

All this while, which to me seemed an eternity but was only a minute, Pa held my hurt hand in his big, soft gentle one. "Your mother told me what happened to your hand," he said quietly, "and how Landon fixed it for you. So now I'm to go into my study and find the glass in my gun case all smashed up, is that it?"

I lowered my eyes. "Yessir. But Andy said he'd fix it."

"We can't always fix what we ruin, Claire Louise," he said softly.

"I know."

"It seems to me that you've done some things around here that can't be fixed. Is that true? I've heard you've behaved right badly."

I shifted my weight. "Pa, can't you scold later? I'm powerful hungry and I have things to tell you and Mama."

For a moment I saw a glint of amusement in his blue eyes. But only for a moment. He said all right. He said he was about starved, too. And we all ought to have some good vittles and more coffee.

He said he could scold even better on a full stomach.

So we ate fresh-baked bread and ham and cheese and tomatoes and pickles and coffee. And I told them what Mr. Swords had said about how the white flags were going up tomorrow and there was going to be a truce. I told them how glad he was to get my wallpaper, and how he said I could have my own edition of tomorrow's paper, that he was saving it for me.

Chip came then, to bring Mercer home to the stables, and Pa settled in. Mama took him into their room and made him take off his uniform and washed him and got him into his nightshirt and robe and slippers and then got some quinine for the fever. Then she settled him in a comfortable chair in the "parlor" with a blanket around him.

Then came the shelling again, all around us. Mama put James, with Sammy, down for a nap and the cave became quiet. I picked up one of Landon's Dickens books when Pa called me softly to him.

I went and he sat there looking sad and gestured that I should sit on a footstool next to him.

He rested his left arm across his middle, set his right elbow on it, and ran the fingers of his right hand across his forehead. "We have to talk about this, Claire Louise. What happened between you and Landon?"

There it was, what I was afraid of. I shrugged my shoulders and said lightly, "Just a stupid argument, Pa."

He shook his head, no. "If you lie, I have to punish you. I have to take you home and make you stay in the cellar alone for a week. Don't think I won't do it. If you tell me the truth, we'll work it out."

Of a sudden I got scared. Alone in the cellar for a week? I couldn't stand that. Pa knew I couldn't. I'd die! What was he about here?

What could I do?

I studied on it for a moment. Pa was a Confederate and a major. It was his army Robert had harmed. If I told him, he might feel honor bound to report to his superiors who had lost Lee's order. The Confederates would give chase to Robert. But then, Landon had said Robert wouldn't go to Jackson, but onward, west. And the war wasn't over yet. There was no time to look for Robert. He had plenty of time to disappear.

"I'm waiting, Claire Louise."

I breathed in deeply. "It's on account of Robert," I told him.

He knew nothing of Robert, except what Mama had likely told him of his staying here. I had to start at the beginning and tell him. He listened, never taking his eyes from my face. And when I got to the part where I gave Robert Jewel and saw him off, he closed his eyes for a second, as if it was all too much to absorb.

"And you never told Landon that it was you who let him go?"

"Nosir."

"Don't you think Landon knows?"

"Yessir. But he just wanted me to say it. To tell him. I don't know why."

"He wanted the truth from you, Claire Louise. His life is based on honor, and he expects it from everybody else. He's caught in the trap of his own honor. It's a terrible thing, honor. It's a lonely thing."

"I want to go and see Landon, Pa. Please, can I?"

"No. He set the rules. Let him run the show. Let him find the way out."

"He doesn't want a way out. He says we'll never be friends again."

"He's too stern with you. I'll have to speak with him."

"No, Pa, please."

He raised his eyebrows. "I know you love your brother, but it'll wait. It's waited this long."

"It can't wait, Pa. I have to go. Either today or tomorrow."

He scowled. "Do you have another fish to fry that I don't know about, young lady?"

"I can't tell you," I said.

"Well then, it's the cellar again."

"No, Pa, please. I can't. I'd die down there. You know I would."

"Yes, I think I do. And this time no Landon to rescue you. Oh, I know how he used to rescue you. Used to come to me and plead that I let you out. It's my only negotiating tool, Claire Louise. So what's it to be?"

"I think you're mean," I said.

"Not as mean as I could be, and you know it. Now I'm getting a headache, so tell me about this other fish you're about to fry."

So I told him then about Sarah. And how she lay in that hospital bed and nobody but me knew she was there. And I told him about the amputated arm and the argument she'd had with Landon and how she was planning on taking the train and running away within the next two days. "Oh, please, Pa, I've got to tell Landon. Don't you see?"

He saw. He went silent. And solemn. He bit his bottom lip. He looked at me quizzically. He thought. He looked at me some more.

"I have to give you this one, Claire Louise," he said. "This time you're right on track, child."

"You mean, you'll let me go?"

He shook his head, no. "Not alone, no. Never alone. Do you know what it's like out there? All those soldiers hearing about a possible truce? Some about to cheer, some about to cry? All about to be out of their heads? And here comes a pretty young girl on horseback? Hey, what say we have some fun? No, sweetie, I go with you."

"But you're sick!"

"Not as sick as I'd be if something happened to you."

"Oh, Pa." I reached up and hugged him. "Pa," I said, "you *do* love me."

He hugged me back. His face, against mine, was warm, but not hot. "What kind of a thing is that to say? You ever have reason to doubt it?"

"Sometimes I thought you didn't," I admitted. Tears came out of my eyes. I wiped them away.

"You need to grow up," he said, "that's your trouble. Now do we have any powders for headaches in this place?"

"Landon left some. He brought them in from your surgery. Do you know I helped there sometimes, Pa?"

"That's the kind of thing I want to hear."

"Then you go for a nap and by tomorrow morning you'll be lots better."

"Thank you, Dr. Claire Louise," he said.

CHAPTER EIGHTEEN

T HERE WAS no shelling the next morning.

"They must have run out of ammunition," Pa said at breakfast. "The cannonading was hot and heavy until the wee hours this morning. As if the enemy was trying to get in their last shot."

Chip came into the hall. "Suh?"

"Yes, Chip."

"When I was acomin' here wif your horses, some man come runnin' over to me and axe me to give this to you all." He handed Pa a copy of the *Citizen*.

"Oh!" I jumped up from my chair. "That's the issue from my wallpaper! Mr. Swords promised it to me!"

Pa was reading the page. It proposed a cease-fire, from Grant to Pemberton. An armistice for several hours. "A flag of truce will be sent out."

"I done seen the white flag on our fortifications," Chip said.

"Then there will be no shelling to worry about," Pa said. "C'mon, Claire Louise. Finish your breakfast and let's get started."

*   *   *

OUT IN the streets our "brave boys" came out from their holes, emerging from their hiding places, from their lines, standing tentatively, like gray owls come out in the day, blinking at the azure sky and the sun, surprised that it all was still there.

Were these conjectures about a truce true? Dared they come out in full and show themselves without getting blown into next week?

Several of them saluted Pa as we rode by. Several of them asked, "Sir, is it true? Is it a truce? Sir, tell us what's going on."

Pa's smile was indulgent, as if they were all Landons. "Wait just a bit," he said, "and we'll all see. But I don't think there will be any firing today."

They'd cheer and mount the Confederate fortifications. Opposite them, only a few yards away, the line of men in blue would emerge from their hiding places from which they had been firing, look across at the men they had been trying to kill, and pick up the cheer.

Pa and I rode on. I had Robert's horse, who was still limping somewhat, so we took our time traveling the fifteen miles to Milliken's Bend hospital. By the time we got to the sprawling affair of brick and tents, I was starting to get a little queasy. And Pa was not looking so good either.

"We should have stopped to rest," I told him. "You don't look so good, Pa."

"I'll ask Landon for a place to lie down," he said.

We reached a side entrance of the tented part of the hospital. Pa dismounted and leaned against Mercer. "Go and find Landon," he instructed me.

I hadn't envisioned it like this. I had assumed Pa would seek out his son and have pleasant words with him and then slip in the conversation that, oh yes, by the way, Claire Louise is here to see you.

The first person I met was a nurse, a woman nurse, middle-aged with a pleasant smile, carrying some clean linens. "Miss," I said, "can you tell me where to find Dr. Corbet?"

"He's in the next tent," she said. "Who needs him?"

"His father is here. Outside. And his father is Major Corbet and not so well. And it's very hot outside. Could I please bring him in?"

"Here, hold these," and she handed me the linens and went outside and came back with Pa in hand. "Right here, sir. On this cot. There you are. You can just lie here and I'll fetch your son in a minute. Oh, I see by your insignia that you're also a doctor. On medical leave, are you?"

"Look here." Pa started to get up. "I didn't come for treatment. You people are busy enough. If you'll just get me some quinine and water, I'll be right as rain."

"I can't do that, sir. I can't administer medicine without the doctor's permission. Now you just lie back. Why, Dr. Corbet will have my head if I dispense medicine without asking him first. Please don't get me in trouble."

Pa smiled. "All right. Wouldn't want the good doctor to give you what for. Claire Louise, go outside and see to the horses. Give them water and put them in some shade."

"There's a trough of water at the end of the lane," the nurse told me, "and a stable boy to put your horses under the trees."

I thanked her and went outside.

I made myself take extra time with the task. I was still upset about seeing Landon and needed more time to gather myself in. Then, finally, when I could stall no more I went back to the tent.

Landon was just straightening up from leaning over Pa. He'd covered him with a light sheet. He turned around and saw me. "You did right by bringing him in," he said. "But why didn't you take him to Dr. Balfour?"

He was making some notations on a chart.

Might as well let it all out at once. "He didn't come for help," I said. "He came to accompany me. He wouldn't let me come alone."

His expression didn't change. He nodded slightly. "Miss Tyler, can you give us some privacy for a moment please?"

"Yes, sir."

He turned to look back at me, then gestured that we should move away from Pa's hearing. We stood, a few feet apart. "So," he said.

I said nothing. I was tongue-tied.

"We aren't old yet, which was the next time we were supposed to be talking. Though I feel like it. I haven't slept all night. Last thing I need to see is you here. What's wrong at home?"

"Nothing."

"Ma all right?"

I nodded yes.

"You have something to say, say it. And it better be important or I'll run you out of here. I'm busy as hell and I haven't time for nonsense."

I felt stung, as if he'd slapped me. So this is what honor did to you. "It is important," I said. My voice had tears in it. I hoped he wouldn't notice, but he did. He looked down, shamefaced, at his chart.

"Well?" This time the voice was more gentle.

How do I say it? "I thought you would want to know. Sarah is home."

He did not even blink. "All right. You've told me. Thank you. But why does that merit a trip here in the severe heat with a sick pa?"

He was starting to turn away. *I was losing him. I mustn't lose him.*

I must talk fast, hit him with it like a Parrott gun. "She's in Dr. Balfour's hospital. She has one arm amputated at the elbow. She got hit with shell fragments at McConnellsburg, near the end of June, and they kicked her out of the army."

He'd already started to walk away. Now he stopped and turned. I saw his face change, as if somebody had punched him in the stomach.

"Did you tell her you were coming to tell me?"

"She doesn't want anybody to know she's here. Especially not you. She said she's going to sneak out of the hospital and leave on the Vicksburg and Jackson Railroad in the next two days. Says she's going to Raymond, to an aunt."

"Raymond, hey?"

"Yessir."

"Don't call me sir."

"No. I, well, I'm so used to Pa now."

He nodded, understanding. He looked over toward Pa. Then back at me. I could see he was calculating. "You fit to ride back to the city?"

Now he sounded like my old Landon. I nodded yes.

"We'll leave Pa here. Grab yourself a sandwich. Miss Tyler will show you where. And some juice. I'll see my superiors and explain things."

I started to walk toward Miss Tyler, but something bothered me.

Was that it? Was that all it took? Was he just going to pick up on things the way they used to be? Like Mama picked up a stitch on her crocheting when she missed one? Nothing was mended. Not as far as I was concerned. Wasn't there something he should do, like stitch up my heart, maybe, the way he'd stitched up my hand?

"Oh," he said, "one more thing."

I turned to look at him. He was taking off his white apron, which did have a considerable amount of blood on it.

"Come here."

I hesitated a moment.

"Well, come *here*."

He held out his arms and I went to him. He enfolded me in a hug that stitched up my heart and everything else that was torn and hurting.

"I've missed you," he said.

"Me too," I told him.

His face grazed the side of mine as he let go. "I'm sorry I lost you Robert," I told him.

"No you're not." He touched the side of my face. "You're a sweet kid and you did what sweet kids do. And if we had more of you there wouldn't be any wars. Only please, don't ever tell anybody you did it."

I promised I wouldn't.

There were tears welling in his eyes. "I'm sorry I was so bad to you." He kissed me. "It was brave of you to come here and face up to me today to give me back Sarah. Because of you, we'll likely be wed. Now go," he said, "we have lots to do together."

I went. Now I was mended. Better than when he'd stitched up my hand.

CHAPTER NINETEEN

I T WAS a long fifteen miles back to Vicksburg. I fed Jeffrey before we left, and when Landon examined his leg, he said the horse was fit to make the trip home. The heat had abated somewhat, still Landon called for a halt near a stream halfway home, and we got off our horses and let them water.

He sat on some grassy ground, so I did, too. His spotless blue uniform looked out of place in the midst of all the greenery. Once seated, he handed me a flask. I just stared at him. He smiled. "It's water," he said.

I took some, surprised at how thirsty I was, handed back the flask, and said, "Thank you." He gulped the rest. Water ran down his chin. He hadn't had time to shave and he wore yesterday's beard.

"What will happen to Pa?" I asked.

He didn't answer for a moment. Just stared straight ahead. "I'll keep him with me until I can properly diagnose him and devise a system of treatment. Likely it'll be quinine, but I have to decide how many grains. I think they'll honorably discharge him."

I nodded. "Then he can come home?"

"Yes, but he'll have to be looked after."

"I can do that."

"No. You have to go back to school. Besides, Ma wouldn't let anybody but herself do it. You can help her when she needs it."

I nodded.

"And he'll still be head of the family. We can't take that away from him."

I nodded again.

He stood up. "We'd best get on." He brushed off his trousers and put on his hat. He stood tall, sure of himself, as he helped me on Jeffrey then reached for Rosie's reins.

It still wasn't the way it used to be with us, I told myself. He was still a bit standoffish. But maybe that's just what the army had done to him. I don't know. Only time will tell. It was suppertime when we arrived in town.

We reined in on the main street. It was crowded with people, soldiers and civilians, who had come to find out what was happening and if there truly would be a surrender of the town tomorrow.

But it was silent, so silent. Nobody in the whole town was speaking, it seemed, just walking slowly about, here and there, some in gray uniform and some in blue, casting suspicious glances at one another, trying to figure if firing would begin again.

Landon and I just sat our horses and watched for a few minutes. Then Landon spoke, in a voice full of authority. "Why don't you men get back to your positions until you're told what to do," he suggested.

They looked at him. They saw his blue coat. His rank.

"Sir," some said. "Yes, sir," from others, even those in gray. "We gonna fight again, sir?" one asked. And "I'se powerful tired, sir."

"I know, I know," Landon replied. "So why don't you all go and get your rest."

They dispersed. So did the civilians. The hospital where Sarah lay was uphill. Landon looked at me.

"I'se powerful tired too, sir," I teased him.

"I was going to suggest you get home to Mama and tell her about Pa and that he'll likely be holed up at Milliken's Bend for a couple of days," he said. "And get some food and sleep. But I don't want you to think I want to get shed of you. You can come with me to find Sarah if you wish."

He was being polite. Of course he wanted to get shed of me. He and Sarah were going to have a romantic reunion. "I think I'll be going home to Mama," I said.

He nodded his head. "Thank you. Tell Ma I'll be by in the morning, before I go back to Milliken's Bend. And that I'd like a huge breakfast."

"I will." I turned Jeffrey in the direction of the caves.

"Claire Louise."

"Yes?"

"The surrender will likely be tomorrow. Tell Ma to get ready to move back to the house. And another thing."

"What?"

"You've grown up, sweetie. I just want to tell you that."

Then he wheeled Rosie around and headed up the hill.

THE NEXT morning was the Fourth of July. A different kind of Fourth than we always had in Vicksburg. At ten o'clock I stood on the sidelines with my hand gripping that of my brother James, watching the ceremonies. Across from us and surrounding us were neighbors and friends, also standing in quiet disbelief, witnessing the arrival of our own troops as they came, in formation, down the street, looking pale but stoic.

Behind us, from the courthouse cupola, the Stars and Stripes waved against the azure sky. A band on the courthouse steps played "Hail Columbia."

Our troops marched down the street in formation. The soldiers were dusty, and some had tears coming down their faces. When they got to the place where the men in blue stood, they surrendered their rifles, sidearms, cartridge boxes, bayonets, knapsacks full of cartridges, every - thing at the feet of the blue soldiers who stood in front of them.

Some kissed their muskets before they set them down.

Some hesitated, as if they could not bear to give them over, and then set them down.

There were no taunts from the Federal soldiers. No cheers. It was all silence, like a rehearsed ballet: march, set down the arms, turn, go back, make room for the next fellow.

There was some sobbing from the onlookers. But it was kept at a minimum.

"Why are people crying?" James asked me.

"Because the fight in our town is over and we must surrender."

"Does that mean there won't be any more shelling?"

"Yes."

"And I can go outside and play with Sammy again?"

"Yes."

"And not worry about anybody taking him to eat him?"

"Yes, James. The Yankees are giving us lots of food."

"Then I don't see why people are crying. We're going back to our own home and I can play outside with Sammy and there won't be any more of Porter's bombs knocking the glass out of houses. What's the matter with people, anyway?"

"I wish I knew, James. I wish I knew."

"Claire Louise, when Landon marries Sarah, will he still love us?"

"Of course."

"He'll still take me on his lap and tell me stories?"

"Yes, if you're good."

"But he'll have to hold Sarah on his lap, won't he? Isn't that why men marry women? So they can hold them on their laps?"

"Yes."

"Where will he get the time for me?"

"He'll make the time, James."

"Look at that one soldier over there, Claire Louise. I think he has his flag wrapped around him under his shirt. I can see a bit of it hanging out of the back. Why is he wearing his flag?"

I looked. It was true. "Because," I said, and my voice broke a little, "the Yankees will take his flag if they see it. And he wants to keep it."

We both watched carefully, and the soldier from the Tennessee regiment handed over his rifle and all his other accoutrements of war, then turned and marched away. At first I thought the Yankee in charge saw the bit of flag hanging from the man's shirt. He opened his mouth as if to stop the man, then minded himself and said nothing. Both James and I saw it. James looked up at me, smiling.

"Landon would let him go, too, wouldn't he?" he asked.

I nodded my head yes.

Just as I said that I felt a tap on my shoulder. I turned. There stood a tattered and weary-looking drummer boy from the same Tennessee regiment, his drum carried over his shoulder. "Miss," he said carefully, "could you all come heah? Just for a moment?"

I pulled James away with me. As the crowd pushed their way into our place, the drummer took his drum off and looked at me. "Ah don't want to hand over my drum to the Yankees," he explained patiently. "Would you all take it, please. An' keep it?"

He handed the sticks to James and the drum to me. My, it was heavy. I set it on the ground. "I'd be proud to," I said.

He took off his hat and bowed. Now I could see that he was only about twelve. A couple of years younger than I. Yet in his eyes I saw he was years older, that he'd seen things I'd never see if I lived to be ninety. James was staring up at him worshipfully.

"Take good care of it, please," he pleaded. "And git it outa here now."

In the next instant he was gone, disappearing into the crowd.

I looked at James and he at me. "C'mon, James," I said, "let's get home."

CHAPTER TWENTY

I GAVE the drum to James so he, too, could have a remembrance from the war, which went on for two more years. James was seven when General Lee finally surrendered to General Grant at Appomattox Court House in Virginia, and already talking about becoming a drummer boy himself.

I think if the war hadn't ended when it did, he would have run away and done it. He certainly knew how to play that drum. He took lessons from Johnny Wilcox, who'd been a drummer boy in the 2nd Mississippi, the unit Pa was in. Johnny came home with a minie ball in his shoulder, the shoulder he used to support the cord of the drum.

Pa recovered from his camp fever, or whatever it was, and came home from Milliken's Bend after the surrender of Vicksburg to spend some time with us, then went back to serve with the 2nd Mississippi as a doctor again. Landon came home the morning of the surrender of the town to tell us that he and Sarah were to wed in two weeks, and Mama near had kittens.

"How do you make a wedding in the middle of a war?" she said.

"Others are doing it," Landon told her. "Anyway, it's Mrs. Clarke's job, not yours."

Once told that, you'd think that Mama was impeached from the presidency of the United States. The Clarkes came back from Jackson. Mama set to "helping" Mrs. Clarke, and those two women put their heads and hearts together so that the wedding two weeks later lacked nothing.

Of course there was no satin and lace for a wedding dress. But there was the dress Sarah's mother had worn. There was precious little time for a trousseau to be made, but in those two weeks we all pitched in and sewed our eyes out.

There was no Pa to escort Mama, for he was in the Shenandoah Valley with Lee and could not get home. But it seemed like everybody in town came to the church to see the "Yankee doctor" wed. The town was now occupied by Yankee troops. They swarmed around the church outside, and Mama and I both prayed there would be no trouble between them and our own Confederate neighbors.

But there wasn't any. The occasion was too joyous. And when Landon and Sarah came out of church, the Yankee troops formed an arch with their swords for the bride and groom to walk under. My brother looked so handsome, and I was so proud.

I was maid of honor and Amy was bridesmaid. But here is the icing on the cake. Because he couldn't get any of his doctor friends at the hospital off duty that day, Landon made James his best man.

Mama dressed him in his best and he was schooled in what he must do. And so our "little man" stood waiting at the altar with Landon and, when the time came, handed Landon the ring. My heart near burst at the sight of him.

As for the reception afterward, the food was plentiful. There were tureens of terrapin stew, turkeys, deer meat, mounds of mashed potatoes and green vegetables. There was a sculpture made of butter of the bride and groom, which Sarah had made with one hand.

The wedding cake was made by Dr. Balfour's wife.

Landon and Sarah took the Vicksburg and Jackson Railroad to Jackson, then a stage to Raymond. They had only two days. Sarah's aunt, the lady she was supposed to run away to, had her home there. She lived alone and she was going to vacate it so they could have the place to themselves.

Landon had to be back at Milliken's Bend to his post Tuesday morning.

CHAPTER TWENTY-ONE

ONE LOVELY day that fall, I was in our kitchen at home, making an iced cake for supper. Landon, Pa, Mama, and Sarah and James were in the front parlor.

I just happened to look out the back window.

At first I thought I was dreaming. I set down my spoon and rubbed my eyes.

She was still there, in front of the barn doors, just standing and bobbing her head up and down. No, I decided. It couldn't be her. *Could it?*

"Landon?" Why was my voice so scratchy?

"Yes?"

"Could you come in here a minute?"

He came. "Want me to lick the bowl?" he asked. But he came and stood beside me as I peered out the window. I heard his intake of breath. Then, "Holy hell in a hand-basket. How'd she get here?"

We were both out the back door without another word. Cautiously we approached the golden-colored horse with the white mane and tail. "Jewel?" he asked. "Is it you, girl, come to see us? Go ahead, Claire Louise, she's your horse."

Jewel tossed her head and whinnied. The reins shook. She was wearing not only reins but a saddle. *My saddle.* "Jewel, there girl. Do you remember me? It's been a while now, hasn't it. Come here and give me a kiss."

The wildness in her eyes changed, went soft, and she took some steps toward me and I nuzzled her face and put my arms around her. She kissed me.

"Landon, it *is* her."

He was carefully tearing a folded-up note from her saddle, opening it and reading it. "Dear Claire Louise," he read. Then he scanned it quickly and handed it to me, and I read the scrawled masculine handwriting.

"I cannot keep her. She's a fine horse, the best, but she yearns for something else. So I am sending her home. Please let me thank you and say that I shall never forget you and that I shall always love you. Your obedient servant, Robert."

There was a postscript, too. "Oh, yes, the blackberries are very rich this year."

Landon and I stared at each other across the horse's back. I felt a tearing inside me. Landon smiled. "He brought her as far as the stream where the blackberries are," he said.

"Yes." I nodded.

He compressed his lips and said nothing. "So he loves you, eh?"

I didn't answer.

"I know he's my age. Twenty-six. How old are you?"

"Please, Landon."

"No please about it. How old are you?"

"I just turned fourteen."

"What went on between you?"

My mouth went dry. So I lied. "Nothing, Landon." It was a kind lie. Why send my brother into a frenzy when there was nothing he could do about it?

I don't know if he believed me.

"Nothing went on between us, Landon. You must believe me."

He lowered his head and kicked some dirt in the barnyard. "If I didn't, I'd get on Rosie right now and ride after him and call him out. The blackhearted puppy. Comes into our house as a guest and makes moves on my sister."

He kept his head bowed for a full minute, getting his feelings under control. "Just promise me you won't run off with him if he ever decides he wants more of those delicious blackberries, will you?"

I said yes. I promised.

"Because I'd have to turn him in, Claire. Even if the war was over."

His head was still down. I went around Jewel to stand beside him, to comfort him. He'd said we all had to let Pa run the family, but things like this never reached Pa. Landon handled them. We tried to make life as easy for Pa as we could.

I went as close to him as I dared. I touched the white sleeve of his carefully tailored and laundered shirt. "Landon? You can trust me. I'd never run off with anybody. My family means too much to me."

He raised his head and looked at me. "You just want a wedding someday like Sarah and I had."

I smiled. He put his arm around me. "I mean it about Robert. If the no-count hooligan comes within a mile of you I'm turning him in, Claire Louise. Remember that."

Jewel whinnied, reminding us we hadn't even offered her anything to eat since she'd come home. So we brought her into the barn, where we fed and watered her. Landon took off her saddle and reins. I kissed her nose. "Well, you have your horse back," Landon said happily. "Just wish she could talk, is all."

Then we went back into the house and I finished icing the cake and Landon licked the bowl.

EPILOGUE

THE PEOPLE of the town of Vicksburg did not celebrate the Fourth of July the summer of 1864.

They did not celebrate it again for eighty-two years.

It was, after all, not only the birthday of America, it was the day their town surrendered to the Yankees. How could they celebrate?

World War I came and went. World War II followed not too far behind. Men from Vicksburg served and died in both.

On the Fourth of July in 1945, the people of Vicksburg decided it was time to celebrate the birthday of their country again. After all, the country had fought two terrible wars to continue to exist in freedom for everyone.

So two months after V-E Day they brought out their flags and their banners and played "The Star-Spangled Banner" and marched and roasted hot dogs and hamburgers and did all sorts of things that make up the celebration of the Fourth in this country.

After eighty-two years they managed to set aside their sorrow. And if the celebration was a little bittersweet, no one can blame them.

AUTHOR'S NOTE

In a book I used for research for another novel I found a Post-it on which I had scribbled a note to myself, somewhere back over the last five years.

"Vicksburg," it said, "great story for a novel."

What brought me around to doing the siege of Vicksburg this time I cannot recall, but I suppose it was always in that file cabinet in the back of my mind where I go when looking for ideas that have been put on the back burner.

"The town where the people were trapped and lived in caves," I reminded myself, "my readers ought to love that premise."

But research and reading told me the story was so much more than that. This was the town where they named one of their 18-pound cannons "Whistling Dick," where the editor of the *Daily Citizen* kept printing all through the forty-seven-day siege, in spite of being shelled and attacked and running out of newsprint. He printed the paper on the back of old wallpaper.

This is the town where the people could venture out on the streets three times a day: eight in the morning, twelve noon, and eight at night, when the Yankee artillerymen ate their meals.

This is the town where "Old Abe," an American bald eagle and mascot for the 8th Regiment, Wisconsin Volunteers, was wounded. It was Old Abe's job to fly, screeching, over the enemy when his regiment fired at them. I have him being attended here by Landon Corbet, our heroine's doctor brother.

In short, I found so many delicious things happening in Vicksburg that I couldn't not write the book. I have followed history scrupulously and did not have to go far afield to fictionalize, but there are things I made up for the sake of story.

The Corbet family, for instance, is fictional, although there were many families in Vicksburg as gallant and well esteemed and confused as were they. I tried to make Claire Louise as true to her age as was possible. Little James I patterned after my grandson James who is near the same age. The trepidation Claire Louise has around her father is the same as I had around my father all my life. Claire Louise finally, in a way, "connects" with her father. I never did.

She calls him "sir" and her mother "ma'am" because that is the way children in the South addressed their parents in those days.

I had some difficulty, at first, with giving Pa malaria. At first I thought it only came to soldiers who fought in World War II, like my late brother-in-law, but I consulted *Doctors in Blue,* a wonderful book by George Worthington Adams, and discovered that malarial fevers were constant and many during the Civil War—522 cases per 1,000.

Which brings me to the many and wonderful books I used for research that are listed in my bibliography. I wish to thank the many authors who wrote them so people like me could enjoy and use them. I particularly thank the women who penned the hospital books, for my information has been diluted from these.

In particular I am grateful to the personnel at the bookstore of the Eastern National Military Park Service at Vicksburg, Mississippi, especially Nikki Anderson, assistant unit manager, who helped me select research books and got them to me so promptly. The National Park Service has not failed me yet.

It is important to note here that at the same time the siege at Vicksburg was winding down—July 2, 3, and 4—the battle of Gettysburg, Pennsylvania, was raging. The South was defeated at Gettysburg the same day, July 4, that Vicksburg surrendered to General U. S. Grant. No one ever seems to mention this when they speak of Gettysburg. It seems that the siege of Vicksburg is a stepchild in the annals of Civil War history.

I realize, fully, that once my faithful readers finish this novel I am going to receive many many e-mails and letters asking what happened to Claire Louise Corbet. Did she meet Robert again? Did he come back to the stream where the blackberries were? Did she run off with him? My readers always want closure, with everything tied up with a bright red ribbon.

Life is not that way. I don't know what happened to Claire Louise any more than you do. But there are possibilities. In life there are always possibilities. So sit back and make up your own ending. Use your imagination. And if you don't like it, then do it over again tomorrow. That's what writing is all about. And that's why I like it so much.

BIBLIOGRAPHY

Adams, George Worthington. *Doctors in Blue: The Medical History of the Union Army in the Civil War.* Dayton, Ohio: Press of Morningside, 1985.

Alcott, Louisa May. *Hospital Sketches.* Boston: Applewood Books, 1992. Originally published in 1863 by J. Redpath, Bedford, Mass.

Ballard, Michael B. *Vicksburg: The Campaign That Opened the Mississippi.* Chapel Hill: University of North Carolina Press, 2004.

Boileau, Lowell. "Suspicions: The Real Story of Special Orders 191?" *The Lost Order Mystery.* http://www.bhere.com/plugugly/lost/story.html.

Child, Lydia Maria. *The Family Nurse.* Boston: Charles J. Hendee, 1837.

Cotton, Gordon A. *Dr. and Mrs. Balfour at Home,* from the *Letters of Emma Balfour, 1847–1857.* Vicksburg, Miss.: Print Shop, 2006.

Denney, Robert E. *Civil War Medicine: Care & Comfort of the Wounded.* New York: Sterling Publishing Co., 1995.

Grabau, Warren E. *Ninety-Eight Days: A Geographer's View of the Vicksburg Campaign.* Knoxville: University of Tennessee Press, 2000.

Hoehling, A. A. *Vicksburg: 47 Days of Siege.* Mechanicsburg, Pa.: Stackpole Books, 1996.

Jones, Katharine M. *Heroines of Dixie: Spring of High Hopes.* St. Simons Island, Ga.: Mockingbird Books, 1974. Originally published in 1955 by Bobbs-Merrill Co, Indianapolis, Ind.

————. *Heroines of Dixie: Winter of Desperation.* St. Simons Island, Ga.: Mockingbird Books, 1975. Originally published in 1966 by Bobbs-Merrill Co., Indianapolis, Ind.

Pember, Phoebe Yates. *A Southern Woman's Story: A Wry and Realistic Account of Work in a Confederate Military Hospital.* Jackson, Tenn.: McCowat-Mercer Press, 1959. Originally published in 1879 by G. W. Carleton & Co., New York.

U.S. Department of the Interior. *Vicksburg and the Opening of the Mississippi River, 1862–63: A History and Guide Prepared for Vicksburg National Military Park, Mississippi* (National Park Service Handbook 137). Washington, D.C.: Division of Publications, National Park Service, U.S. Department of the Interior, 1986.

Waldrep, Christopher. *Vicksburg's Long Shadow: The Civil War Legacy of Race and Remembrance.* Lanham, Md.: Rowman & Littlefield Publishing Group, 2005.

Werner, Emmy E. *Reluctant Witnesses: Children's Voices from the Civil War.* Boulder, Colo.: Westview Press, 1998.

DATE DUE